THE CYCLONE AND OTHER SHORT STORIES

PALAGUMMI PADMARAJU

Compiled and Edited by
Pradeep Balu

(Grandson of Shri. Palagummi Padmaraju)

Contents

My Sincere Thanks To

Dr.Palagummi Sasidhar
(Nephew of shri Palagummi Padmaraju)

Ms.Palagummi Seetha
(Daughter of shri Palagummi Padmaraju)

Mr.Palagummi Kameshwar Rao
(Nephew of shri Palagummi Padmaraju)

Ms.Palagummi Rathna
(Daughter of shri Palagummi Padmaraju)

Dr.K.Sreenivasa Rao
(Secretary of Sahitya Akademi)

Prof. Y. Sreedhar Murthy
Chairman, The Triveni Foundation (Regd.)

Dr. D. Anjaneyulu
(Writer, journalist, and critic)

Mr.Gopalam Karamchedu
(Writer)

Mr.Suresh Kohili
(Writer, Film historian)

Ms.Sharada
(Australia)

Ms.Shagufa Fathima F
(Senior Publishing Consultant Notion Press)

Prelude To Anthology

- Palagummi Seetha & Palagummi Ratna -

(Daughters of shri Palagummi Padmaraju)

It is with immense pride and heartfelt reverence that we bring forth The Cyclone and Other Short Stories by Shri.Palagummi Padmaraju, an anthology of our father's finest short stories in English. His mastery over storytelling, both in Telugu and English, has left an indelible mark in the literary world, and it is our privilege to present his works to a wider audience.

In compiling this collection, we made a conscious decision to retain the foreword written by Late Shri A.S. Raman, a distinguished journalist, former editor of Illustrated Weekly of India, and a dear friend of our father. More than just an introduction, his foreword is a profound tribute to Shri.Padmaraju's storytelling brilliance, capturing the essence of his literary genius in a way that remains timeless.

Shri A.S. Raman's credentials further validate our choice. A Padma Shri awardee and Fellow of the Lalit Kala Akademi, he was an intellectual and literary connoisseur of great repute. His deep understanding of literature and art makes his reflections on our father's works even more significant.

Our decision to preserve his foreword is also deeply symbolic. In an extraordinary twist of fate, our father's birth anniversary coincides with the day Shri A.S.Raman passed away. This poignant connection strengthens our resolve to honour not just our father's legacy, but also that of a literary luminary who appreciated and celebrated his contributions to literature.

Through this anthology, we hope to introduce a new generation of readers to the magic of Shri.Palagummi Padmaraju, while paying tribute to the literary bond between these two distinguished men.

Foreword

'Gaalivana' delighted everyone

- Shri.A.S. RAMAN-

(Indian writer and journalist and a former editor of the

Illustrated Weekly of India.)

There are four kinds of writers: (i) Those who write for money, (ii) Those who write for a cause, (iii) Those who write for other writers and (iv) Those who, while writing for other writers, manage to impart to their vision and style a pleasing blend of commercialism, idealism and professionalism in the right proportions.

Once a professor of English literature complained to Rabindranath Tagore that style Saratchandra Chatterjee's novels had neither style nor substance. The poet replied: "I write for people like you. But he writes for me." Similarly, Palagummi Padmaraju, who belonged to the fourth category, apparently wrote without style or substance but actually with both, concealed by writing for films, he accepted the challenge of commercialism. By writing about people in the round he gave flesh and blood to his own kind of socialist realism with a human face and by choosing to write in the living language of the present with elan, empathy and elegance, he established a firm rapport with the Avant Garde.

He wrote with a touch of casualness. But there was intense concentration packed into his effort. His cinema connection never destroyed or diluted the quality of his creativity. Here he was in good company viz, Mahakavi Devulapalli Krishna Sastry whose film lyrics stand out for their literary excellence.

I first came to know of Padmaraju in the '30s as a science teacher with his heart elsewhere. Later a friend, closely related to him, showed me with visible pride some of his prose verses written under the initials Paa Pa. Now I knew where his heart was. At once I could identify these verses with a writer who had the intellect of a scientist and the insights of a poet. The quality that struck me in his writing then were its polish, precision and controlled passion. He had already perfected the difficult technique of saying so much by actually saying so little, the technique of the moderns at their best. This technique gradually became synonymous with his work.

The criticism against the bulk of writing in regional languages is that it tends to be too flabby or flamboyant in the absence of exposure to the latest trends in world literature. Writers like Padmaraju and Rachakonda Viswanatha Sastry are exceptions. They are as good as the best of the West, but our purists perhaps dismiss them as square pegs in the round hole. Normally they don't, open! But they accept them with reservations.

So, when Padmaraju's story, Cyclone, won the second prize in the prestigious Herald-Tribune sponsored International Short Story Competition in 1952, I was not surprised. I was then in Delhi. I had many friends among the Hindi writers who had participated in this tough competition. When they read Cyclone in The Hindustan Times, the co-sponsor of the contest in India, they readily conceded that the prize went to the right man. The story delighted everyone by its Chekhovian textures and Shavian twists, cleverly concealed beneath its deceptive blandness. Years later when I read it in Telugu. I could not help suspecting that Padmaraju must have written the story first in English and then translated it into Telugu. Of course, there was no valid reason for my suspicion except my own impression that the English version was so good that it read like an original. It seemed to be too tidy and taut to be treated as a translation. Padmaraju could have become one of our leading writers in English if he had opted for a literary career in the language of Shakespeare, Shelley and Shaw, the trinity he admired most. Whenever he wrote in English-and he often did, though not often enough I never felt that I was reading a writer whose first love was his own mother tongue. His passion for excellence in whatever he wrote enabled him to handle any language with a feeling for form and a commitment to content. He published his first story, Subbi, in English. It appeared in Triveni. The year was 1938. The editor of a highly respected Telugu literary journal read the story in Triveni with a feeling of guilt. For earlier he had rejected its Telugu version.

Cyclone is vintage Padmaraju, I wonder why people did not give him the nickname-Cyclone Padmaraju. His portrayal of Rao and the beggar woman is typically Shavian in its luminous, bitter sweet blend of cynicism, realism and humanism and utterly un-Shavian in its lack of leftist rhetoric. He neither condemns nor condones Rao's perfectly natural craving for the warmth of the woman's embrace nor does he feel sorry for her poverty. One the contrary he seems to approve, however tacitly, of her attempt to run away after stealing Rao's purse and cash from the railway booking clerk's collection box, taking advantage of the confusion and panic caused by the cyclone. The behaviour of Rao and the beggar woman is refreshingly normal and predictable. Padmaraju accepted men and women as he found them. He neither rejected them for their weaknesses nor romanticised them for their strengths. He had the same reverence for both - the saint and the sinner 'To him mankind was not black or white; he saw lovely greys everywhere.

He was the author of nearly 70 compact, well-crafted short stories, several novels, poems, plays and essays. He wrote a lot but published only a little. Though a non-conformist in his literary attitudes if not in his life-style which seemed Bohemian but had a discipline of its own, he managed to impress the establishment. He won the Sahitya Akademi award for his scintillating, and down to earth novel, Nalla Regadi (Black Soil). One of his plays, Rakta Kanneeru (Tears of Blood), was a sensational hit on stage both in Telugu and Tamil. He wrote an immensely popular radio play, Santhi Nilayam (Abode of Peace), in ten parts, He even produced a first detective novel, Chachhi Saadhinchaadu (Accomplished through Death) under gentle but irresistible pressure from his friend, Bujjai, the artist-son of Mahakavi Krishna Sastry. As a poet, according to his own confession, Padmaraju did not have much to say. He tried his hand at poetry apparently under the strong influence of Krishna Sastry, with whom his identification was total. No two persons so sharply different in their temperaments, attitudes and beliefs ever came closer than Krishna

Sastry and Padmaraju, I guess Krishna Sastry loved Padmaraju for his ability and integrity while Padmaraju admired Krishna Sastry for his many splendoured poetic vision as well as for his graciousness and generosity.

Padmaraju was basically an exponent of the rural ethos of the two villages in the West Godavari district, Thirupathipuram and Rayakuduru, where he spent his childhood. Most of his stories have characters drawn from his own nostalgic memories of the people he loved and hated in his childhood- the people with whom he had so much to do when he was under the sweet tyranny of his own dreams and passions, Paddaalu, Pulli and Venkateswarulu, the tailor, were some those he knew intimately in his childhood and he has immortalised them in his short stories. The death of his maternal grandfather moved him so deeply that he used it as backdrop for some of his stories, such as Baalyam (Childhood), Viyyanna Thaatha Maranam (Death of an old man), Gaali Vaana (cyclone), etc. He was a firm believer in the sweet innocence and divinity of children. In his story, Daari Thappina Bussu (The wayward bus), the bizarre pranks of the ghost of Dugganna Senani make no impression at all on Kishtappa and other children who decide to tackle him on their own terms. Overpowered by their charm, the ghost becomes their friend and ensures that the plants and flowers petrified by the touch of adults regain their original form at the touch of the children.

It would be difficult to trace literary influences in Padmaraju's work, because he did not imitate the writers he admired. Many literary stalwarts such as T.S.Eliot, Joyce, Kafka, Shaw etc., had some impact on him. Freud, Marx and other intellectual investigators also moulded his thinking to some extent. But he never followed theories and techniques if they had no relevance to his work. He did not write to illustrate this ism or that. If what he wrote fitted into the literary format of the day, he was happy. If it did not, he was not sorry. So, one should not look for, say, the stream of consciousness or phenomenological perceptions in his writings which enshrine his own personal philosophy and his own personal vision. But he had an open mind, ready to receive influences from all countries. As a South Korean proverb says: "Allow birds to fly over your mind: But make sure that they don't build nests there."

Padmaraju was not only a voracious and discerning reader, with a receptive, with-awake mind, but also interested in science, technology, engineering, electronics and economics. There were tidy compartments in his brain-one for analysis, another for creation, a third for exposition, a fourth for information, and so on. So, he could speak from any platform without making a fool of himself and he would speak coolly and convincingly, without emotion without rhetoric and without gimmicks. Even those close to him did not know what his likes and dislikes were, because of his rational and refined approach to men and matters. He would react to every question with an embarrassed smile which often was his only answer. This does not mean that he was a block of ice. He had warm sentiments, deep involvements and strong feelings. But they rarely surfaced. They remained cosily protected by his tough-not rough-exterior.

He was secretly scared stiff at the thought of death. He feared death no doubt, but he had the confidence that he could fight against it, if only he could anticipate it. When it came, tragically enough, he was not prepared for it. It came like a thief. Unfortunately, he was defenceless against thieves. He had trained himself to deal only with gentlemen.

Foreword

- Pradeep Balu-

**(Compiler & grandson of Shri Palagummi
Padmaraju)**

I take great pride in presenting my grandfather's
short stories in English, originally written in Telugu.

My Grandfather Shri. Palagummi Padmaraju is an
eminent writer and has the credit of taking Telugu
literature to international standards. His story holds a
mirror to our lives, reflecting our struggles, joys, and
the mundane moments that shape us. "The Cyclone
and Other Short Stories" does just that. It captures
the essence of human experience through the lens
of Shri.Padmaraju, a celebrated Telugu writer whose
words resonate even decades after his demise.
Shri.Padmaraju's journey began in Tirupati Puram,
where he encountered the world with curious eyes and
a storyteller's heart. As a Science Lecturer, he balanced
his love for literature with the precision of science,
giving him a unique perspective on life. His writings
weave the cultural tapestries of Andhra Pradesh,
showcasing the richness of Telugu literature while
exploring universal themes of humanity, love, loss, and
resilience.

In this collection, you'll find stories that push you
to question, reflect, and connect. The experiences
Shri.Padmaraju shares are not just his own; they
breathe life into the human conditions of his times,
expecting to encounter characters that feel familiar
who face dilemmas that echo our own.

These narratives honour a legacy that has influenced both literature and cinema in Telugu culture. They remind us that stories matter—they can ignite change and inspire generations. So, as you turn the pages, prepare for moments of introspection. Let Shri.Padmaraju's keen insights guide you through the ups and downs of life. There's magic in simplicity and depth in brevity. The stories unfold gently, challenging you to look deeper and embrace the whirlwind of emotions tied to each tale.

I am blessed to have legendary grandfathers - Shri. Palagummi Padmaraju, Shri.M.G.Chakrapani, Shri. M.G.Ramachandran (former Chief Minister of Tamil Nadu) and Shri.Palagummi Viswanadham.

CHAPTER I

Cyclone

The weather was threatening, and the train was very late. As he entered the second-class compartment, Rao was reminded of the comforts of his well-ordered household, his meticulously neat study, his rosewood writing table with the green-shaded lamp in a corner, his cushioned chair, which had developed very comfortable hollows to the curves of his body, his wife, who sat unobtrusively on the sofa, and his four children, two sons and two daughters, of whom he was very proud. All the three berths in the compartment were occupied, with bedclothes spread on them, and he could sense a feeling of resentment in the four occupants of the compartment even without looking at them. He had half a mind to try another compartment, but the porter had already put his suitcase, his bedroll, and his umbrella on an upper berth, and the train was about to move out. One of the travellers folded his bedclothes a little and made room for Rao to sit. Rao accepted it with half-muttered thanks and began to take stock of things around him. All four, he could see, were long-distance travellers. He saw their shoes pushed under the seats. Odd trousers, coats, and shirts hung on pegs, and the men were all in pyjamas. The two berths near the windows were occupied by two elderly, nondescript men. On the long inner berth sat a young man and a very young woman who were obviously man and wife. The mildly oppressive smell of tobacco smoke, which Rao disliked so much, filled the compartment. Rao had very definite views on smoking in railway compartments. He had very definite views on many things. At fifty, having lived an active and successful life, he could look back with a certain self-satisfaction. As a professional lawyer, he was a practiced speaker of resources, and he liked his own voice. Now that he had retired, he did much public speaking. He was traveling now to address an association that styled itself 'The Club of Theists.' The wind rose and smote the windscreens of the compartment with a dull persistence. It had grown suddenly dark inside. It could not have been evening yet. His neighbour looked up from some crime story he was reading and asked Rao what the time was. Rao considered for a moment, though he had a watch on his wrist, and replied without hurry, "Three, I think." "How very dark it is!" said his companion. Rao did not say anything but scrutinized his face for a moment. He was about the same age as Rao, and Rao wondered how, at his age, he could enjoy reading a crime story. The man looked older than his years, Rao thought. Rao prided himself on his health. His wife looked older than he, and he liked to tell her that many people thought her to be his elder sister or even his mother. He certainly did not look like a father of a 25-year-old son. The son had taken over Rao's legal practice recently. Few people with such a good practice as his retired at his age. All the shutters were by now closed, and the wind was howling outside. A slight drizzle had begun to work its way into the compartment. Everything felt cold to the touch. The young man tried to nestle closer to the young woman, but she looked around the compartment and moved away. The young man lighted a cigarette. The young woman made a grimace and moved farther away from him. The young man smiled and continued to smoke. From the neatly dressed hair of the young woman, a few curls danced about her cheeks and forehead. Rao remembered that he set the style of the hairdo of his daughters.

Their habits, religious beliefs, food, friendships, clothes were all regulated according to his notions of what was seemly. The old man in the corner opposite took out a brown flannel shirt from inside the folds of his bed-clothes. He looked comical, Rao thought, in those striped pyjamas and brown flannel shirt. The old man poured out some hot coffee from a flask. Rao remembered the flask of chocolate milk in his box. He took it out. He was very fond of his chocolate milk but he never took it more than twice a day, a cup each time. It was raining heavily now. The noise of the train was drowned in the howling of the wind. "Looks like a storm," said the young man to his wife. She covered herself with a rug and did not reply. Rao began to be really worried about the weather. At a wayside station, the door of the compartment was suddenly flung open and there was a terrific gush of wind and rain. A woman in tattered, half-drenched clothes came in. Immediately, there was a howl of protest. But the woman quietly closed the door and stood in a corner, her clothes dripping. The old man growled angrily, "Don't you know this is a second-class compartment?" "Oh! my dear grandfather! Do you grudge a poor woman a little room to stand? Kind fathers. Fathers of many children! Spare a poor woman a copper. I am dying of hunger. You are all great, rich people. I know you won't let a poor woman die of hunger. Rao looked at her. He saw in her eyes a twinkle which roused a dull antagonism in his heart. She was about thirty. She did not actually look well-fed, but was certainly not dying of hunger. There was a self-assurance in her, in spite of all her pretence of helplessness. Rao pitied the poor and the socially oppressed but he was against begging on principle.

When the woman approached him, he refused to give her anything with such a finality in his manner that she immediately turned away.

She went to the other side and bent down to touch the feet of the old man. The old man drew them away, laughing a little awkwardly. "Go away. Go away!" he said. "Do not say so, grandfather! You are not as unkind as that father there. He has no pity in his heart. He can say 'No' to a poor, miserable woman like me." The imitation of his 'No' was a piece of impudence, felt Rao, but he could do nothing. He sat observing her in spite of himself, whether to buy his peace with a coin and earn the unexpressed disapproval of his fellow passengers or to let her go on. He was unnecessarily vehement when he asked her again to go away. The beggar woman now began to wail. "I got into this compartment thinking that the rich would not see me faint with hunger. I thought I could get my day's food here. The poor people in the third class are more generous. They will not scold, nor be harsh on, a poor woman for begging. They know what I suffer, and they have pity in their hearts. . ." She had become the center of interest. Rao's neighbour stopped reading his crime story and looked at her. His interest was roused. "Where are you from?" he asked her. "Nowhere, my kind father. Rich people like you belong somewhere. You have big houses from which beggars are turned away by your servants. A poor woman like me has nowhere to call her own." "She has a very sharp tongue," he said to Rao in English. "Do not scold

me in English, Father. I am a poor, wretched woman."
It was very dark outside. The wind was gathering
more strength. The train moved very slowly. Rao was
nearing his destination. He was hoping some members
of the Theists Club would be at the station. It was
going to be a problem getting his things out. The
wind roared outside like an angry ocean. He could
hear the crash of falling trees. The beggar woman
sat facing the young couple. She began, "There is my
little mother here. And there is the little father too.
Little mother! Have pity on this poor woman and ask
Father to spare me a coin. Why do you turn away like
that? Has my little mother had a quarrel with my little
father? Little Father smokes too much. Little Mother
should not allow it. Ah! My little mother is smiling."
"Give her something and send her away," said the
young woman. "I know my little mother is very kind-
hearted. Now grandfather will also give me something.
I should not have annoyed him. I know he is a very
kind man. Everybody gave her something except Rao.
They were all amused by her talk. But Rao's mind was
preoccupied. He was thinking of the storm and his
approaching destination. The train had stopped. Rao
did not know it for some moments. Umbrella in hand,
he got up and opened the door. The wind threw him
back with such force that he almost fell down. The
beggar woman offered to carry his things down. He
did not stop her. He ran across the platform into the
shelter of the station. The beggar woman staggered
with the burden of his luggage behind him and put his
things in the waiting room. There was not a single light
anywhere in the station. He took some money out and
offered it to the woman. She did not actually refuse
it but said something that he could not make out and
was gone the next moment. He felt dazed and went

into the waiting room, his mind a blank. It was difficult to keep one's foothold in that wild screeching wind. All his clothes were wet. He mechanically opened his box, fumbled in it, and came upon a torch. He was almost beside himself with joy. He had no notion that there was a torch in his box; he had no notion about anything. He changed into warm clothes, wore a woollen pullover, wrapped his flannel muffler round his head and ears, and thus fortified himself against the cold.

He sat in the chair forgetting to lock his box, trying not to realize the predicament he was in. He saw the light of the train moving and it occurred to him that there must be somebody in the station. He came out and saw two figures trying to cross the platform. He raised his voice and called out. The figures stopped. He approached them and saw that one of them was the station master and the other a porter. "I have to go into the town," Rao frantically told them. "Impossible. The road is blocked, every inch of it, with fallen trees. Everything has gone out of order, the telegraphic communications, the electric power supply, everything. You will have to spend the night in the waiting room. The train will stop at the next station for the night. We received a message that the cyclone will be very heavy and that it will last for nearly 36 hours." "But there is nobody else in the waiting room." "I can't help it. You will have to make the best of it.' The station master moved away. Rao went back into the waiting room and dropped into an easy chair in utter despondency. It did not occur to him that he might as well close the door of the room through which wind and rain were rushing in. Two window panes had already blown off. A nameless fear seized him and the agony of it was unbearable. There was not a soul around. The bleakness of the railway station and the fury of the cyclone gripped him with the terror of a nightmare. Suddenly he felt a presence in the room. He saw a vague shape flowing in through the open doorway. He switched on his torch and saw the completely drenched shivering figure of the beggar woman. Her wet hair clung to her face and water streamed down the loose strands. "Why didn't you close the door? You could have been warm," she said at the top of her voice to make herself heard. He got up mechanically and tried to close the door. She helped him. But the wind beat with redoubled fury and the bolt gave way. They closed the door again and pushed the furniture in the room, a massive table, two chairs and a chest of drawers, against it. Rao wondered why it had not occurred to him earlier to close the door. He felt a little more, safe and warm. There was a terrific crash somewhere nearby. "Something has fallen. Perhaps it is a part of this building itself. What a storm! I have never seen anything like it," the woman said. There was not a trace of fear in her voice and he wondered at her assurance. He turned the light towards her and saw her crouching in a corner, shivering. He opened his box and took out one of his dhotis. He threw it to her saying, "You better change into this." She could not hear him but was grateful for the warm dhoti. She changed into it and again sat down in the corner. Rao felt hungry. He took out a packet of biscuits. He looked at the hazy figure in the corner. It occurred to him that she may also be hungry. "Will you have some biscuits?" He asked her. "What did you say?" she shouted. Their voices were drowned by the howling of the wind. He drew closer to her and gave her a few biscuits. "This is all I have," he said, as though in apology. He went back and sat on his suitcase. He felt a little easy because of her presence. She was better than no company and she appeared perfectly at peace with herself. She took things for granted, even the cyclone. She was used to the rough and tumble of life, he thought. Rao looked at his watch and saw that it was only nine. It had seemed that he had been there for ages. He should have gone on to the next station, he told himself. It had not occurred to him that he was getting down at a small wayside station. The town was nearly two miles away and he could have reached it from the next station also. A sudden fear paralyzed his mind.

The building might collapse, and the only way out of it was blocked by a barricade of furniture. In panic, he ran to the woman and asked, "Do you think this building will come down?" "Who can say? It looks strong enough, but the cyclone may be stronger." What she said was far from reassuring, but her tone was warm and cajoling. He went back to his box. She moved into the corner near him. She told him, "I cannot hear you from there." "I never knew a cyclone could be so terrible," he said. "Don't you worry," she said. "There are two of us instead of one. That damned ticket collector actually pushed me out of the train as it was moving. That's how I am here. Still, I have no regrets. You gave me something warm to wear and something to eat. I might have done worse had I gone on. One has to take things as they come. What is the good of worrying?" The monotone of her voice was vaguely comforting. He abhorred her physical presence, yet he began to feel grateful for her company. "Have you any relations?" he asked her, half annoyed at himself for the intimacy of the question. She moved a little closer to him to avoid speaking loudly. "Everybody has relations," she said, "but what use is it? My father drinks all the time, and they say he murdered my mother. I was never actually married, but I have two children by a rogue who does nothing but drink and gamble. I feed the family. The two children are too young to learn begging. My man spends four annas out of my earnings on drink every day. But he is mortally afraid of me. He drinks to overcome his sense of shame when he has to face me." "What do you earn a day?" "Some days I earn as much as five rupees, but not often. Few people refuse me a copper. I know I have a way with them." Rao involuntarily focused the light on her face and saw that she was smiling. She would not think twice about giving her body to an utter stranger, he thought, still looking at her smiling face. "Why do you look at me like that?" she asked. "I am not as pretty as I once was." He hated her for the suggestion. "I am not looking at your face," he said, "I had forgotten to switch off the torch." Suddenly there was a terrific crash. The barricade of furniture scattered in all directions, and the door flung open. One panel came off its hinges. Rao clutched at the beggar as if she were his last support. A little mortified, he was himself in a moment. But he allowed her to lead him to another corner beside the open door where the wind was not so fierce. She made him sit down, huddled herself beside him, and threw her arms round him, casually and naturally. He was comforted by the animal warmth of her embrace.

"Sit closer and put your arms around me," she said, "you will feel warmer. Poor old father, you are shivering all over." She nestled closer into his lap, and he felt her warm breast against his knee. She went on talking. "This corner is the safest. Father has lovely young daughters of whom he is thinking now. My hut must have blown off. What may have happened to my two children? I hope my neighbours will help. My man is not good. He must be dead drunk." Rao was not listening. He was only aware of her warm body. He choked her in his embrace, full of frenzy and anguish. She patted him gently on his thigh as though to say she understood it all. Gradually his mind ceased to work. A numbness came over Rao's feet, and he was again conscious of his surroundings. He shifted to a more convenient position without disturbing the woman. He switched on his light and looked at her. She was asleep. Her face was pure and innocent in repose.

The cyclone's fury had not lessened. But he felt very calm and very tired. He fell asleep. When he woke up, the rain had stopped, but the wind was still high. The beggar woman was gone. The day was breaking. He looked at his watch and saw that it was already five. He stood up and his knees ached. He felt his pockets. His purse was missing. He could not bring himself to believe that the beggar woman had robbed him. Maybe he had lost it in the confusion of the night. He looked for it in the room and then came out onto the platform. There were signs of destruction all over the place. Some people possibly from the town, were approaching along the railway embankment. At the farther end of the station lay some injured persons. He looked at them from a distance and instinctively recoiled, He had never been face to face with so much human pain. The booking office had collapsed. Cupboards, tables, chairs and other furniture lay helter-skelter. He stood there blindly looking at the wreckage. It was still dark inside. As his eyes grew accustomed to the half-light, he saw a figure lying motionless under the wreckage.

He flashed his light in that direction. It was the beggar woman. He staggered. He bent down and touched her forehead. She was cold and lifeless. The lower part of her body had been crushed. In one of her hands, he saw his purse. In the other, there were a few coins and currency notes, evidently from the booking clerk's chest. The clerk must have left in a hurry, the previous night. He bent down and kissed her forehead, again and again. He lived and relived through every trivial moment of the night. There lay that dear creature who had given him so much comfort and assurance through the cyclone. There she lay, a victim of that very cyclone. He did not have it in him to blame her for stealing his purse, or raiding the booking office. He felt that he understood her.

She had touched the inmost chords of human warmth in him. Not even his wife, nor any of his children, had ever come so near to him as this poor beggar. There was the sound of approaching voices. He stood thinking for a brief moment. Then, with a sudden resolution, he loosened her fingers, took away the money, and put it in the open drawer. He could not bring himself to take his own purse back. He must leave her something that belonged to him. Carefully he removed the card bearing his name from the purse and walked away.

Translated by Shri Palagummi Padmaraju
(Rendered from the original story Gaalivaana in
Telugu)
Published by Sahitya Akademi—1986

Trivia:

Gaalivana (Cyclone) is a story written by renowned story writer and film maker Palagummi Padmaraju.

Gaalivana (Cyclone) won the second prize in an international competition organized by the New York Herald Tribune in 1952. The story Gaalivana (Cyclone) was first published in the Sunday edition of Andhra Patrika on 13 May 1951, and was republished in the same magazine on 19 March 1952. The story won the New York Herald Tribune Award and has been translated into several languages around the world, thus taking Telugu literature to international standards.

NEW YORK
Herald Tribune

A European Edition is Published Daily in Paris

PEnnsylvania 6-4000   230 West 41st Street, New York 18

March 21, 1952

Mr. Palagummi Padmaraju
W.G.B. College
Bhimavaram, Madras State
India

Dear Mr. Padmaraju:

It was a great pleasure when I heard that your story, "Cyclone," was among those selected for an award in the New York Herald Tribune's World Prize Story contest.

In combination with the enclosed check, I want to send you my warmest congratulations on your achievement.

I am confident, from the world-wide response to this competition, that the result will be a greater interest in short-story writing and a general improvement in the art everywhere. The fact that your story is among those which achieved the very highest level of distinction should be a source of deep satisfaction to you.

Please accept my best wishes for your continued success.

Sincerely yours,

NEW YORK HERALD TRIBUNE SYNDICATE

Willet Weeks
Manager

amr
enclosure

TELEGRAMS: ANDHRAPATRIKA.
TELEPHONE: № 2544.

The Andhra Patrika

7. THAMBU CHETTY STREET.
POST BOX № 212.

FOUNDED. 1908.
Madras.

March 13, 1952.

My dear Padmaraju Garu,

    You will have received my wire of this morning. My heartiest congratulations to you. We are all proud of your achievement. In fact, every Andhra must be proud of it. I have particular right to be happy because the Andhra Patrika is associated in organizing the competition and a friend of mine got the prize. You have brought a place for Telugu story in the World Literature. May this be a beginning for further achievements by you and by others. I will make the announcement in tomorrow's paper as per the instructions given by the Hindustan Times. I enclose herewith a copy of the communication received from the Hindustan Times.

    Please let me know when you are likely to come to Madras so that we want to have a small function in your honour.

    Please send a message for publication.

With best wishes,

Yours sincerely,

(S. SAMBHU PRASAD.)
Editor.

P. Padmaraju, Esq.,
Lecturer,
Bhimavaram College,
BHIMAVARAM,
(W.Godavary Dt.,)

CHAPTER II

Subbi

After a pleasant tour in the summer vacation with some of his friends, Jagannadha Rao came home for only a week's stay before having to go back to college. He was the only son of his old parents, and it was not just his sense of duty that brought him home but also his innate desire to be in his native village for however short a time, for he knew he was always happy with his father and mother.

A youth in his early, inconsolable twenties, he had been experiencing a strange malady, and this malady gripped him rather firmly. The one thing that worried him most was that, while many of his classmates were married, had wives, and some had children too, and had houses of fathers-in-law as a vacation resort, with all the consequent excitement, and if nothing else, the excitement of having plenty to eat and nothing to do, his own father most disconcertingly turned away every match that came his way, however beautiful the girl and however tempting the dowry. One day he actually approached his father with a pretence purely of being disgusted with this uncouth treatment meted out to his prospective fathers-in-law and said, "Father, why not accept some match or other? Everybody seems to think we are waiting for a bigger dowry." His father smiled good-humouredly, as if accepting that the conjecture was not far wrong, puffed away the seriousness of the situation with his cigar smoke, and asked, "Where is the hurry?" Then twitching his eyebrows into a more serious pose, he took another puff at the cigar and added, "We can wait till your education is finished. Can't We?"

Jagannadha Rao could not proceed any further without letting out his own secret anxiety to get married, and he was by no means inclined to do this. So, he said, "You know best, Father," and left it there—though he had no doubt at all that in this matter it was he himself who knew best. The mere sight of a woman was enough to disturb him.

He became awkwardly self-conscious whenever he met one. Unending was his toilet every day. When he dressed to go out, he would adjust the folds of his dhoti several times, take care to raise the collar of his shirt, and look into his face in the mirror to make sure which expression of the lips would lend an air of seriousness to his person. He would walk uneasily in the street, fearing that others might deem his gait inartistic. He never doubted that every girl was scanning him with her eyes from head to foot, was observing the colour of his shirt, and his manner of wearing the dhoti... And now there was Subbi, who seemed always to look at him with devouring eyes. He knew Subbi from her very childhood. She was an orphan girl brought up on the verandah of his house. He remembered her mother, a servant of his household, who died when this girl was barely three years old. Subbi herself had been a very faithful servant of the household for some time now, and nothing about her had hitherto struck him as noticeable or peculiar. But now there was a difference. Subbi had grown up! And he was actually attracted by her! He would gaze perturbed at her beautiful limbs that seemed to swell out of her insufficient rags. He knew she was taking notice of him. Of course, she did not smile or screw up her left eye mischievously, as he read of more well-bred girls doing. But he was sure of this: she looked up to him with profound respect and admiration. She was incapable of showing anything more than admiration in her eye, young, foolish, and untrained in such situations as she was.

One evening, his father had gone to some neighbouring village on his business, and his mother was busy in the kitchen. Subbi was all alone in a secluded corner of the house with a heap of rice before her, picking out small stones. Jagannadha Rao made bold and went near her. She looked up at him and then timidly let down her eyes. He felt encouraged and touched her on her bare shoulder. Both of them experienced a sudden thrill coursing through their bodies. At that moment he fancied that he heard some noise outside and hurriedly came out. But as he found nobody there, he mustered courage and went in again. As for Subbi, nobody had touched her on her bare shoulder so tenderly, and the sensation was by no means unpleasant. She yielded. Soon the vacation came to a close, and Jagannadha Rao returned to his college. Subbi was not intelligent enough to look deeper than into the immediate future. She knew only two things: firstly, that she should keep secret as long as she could the fact of her having conceived; and secondly, that she should attend to her daily duties despite the strain it meant to her in her condition.

But she could not conceal the fact of her being pregnant. She did not know what to do with the increasing evidence that her body put forth. This became unmanageable, and everybody could see clearly what the matter with her was. Rathamma, Jagannadha Rao's mother, called her one day to her room and asked her, with more than motherly tenderness, "Tell me who it is that seduced you, you foolish girl. Tell me his name. We shall force him to make amends for what he has done to you." By now, Subbi understood another thing: that she should only weep without muttering a single word when anybody was so kind as to question her regarding this affair!

The news soon spread like smoke, but nobody connected Jagannadha Rao's name with Subbi's affair. He had been in the village only for a week, and nobody even remembered that he had been there this vacation. When Subbi began to weep, Rathamma's tender feelings were touched, and she patted the unfortunate girl and asked her not to weep and almost assured her that she need fear nothing. The good old lady approached her husband and told him all about poor Subbi. Venkayya was alarmed at this information and hurriedly said, "Send the wretch away from the house and be done with it. The jade! She ought to have known better." Rathamma pleaded, "You see that she is an innocent, poor little thing. And what is the use of driving her out? She would only get more lost. Some vagabond has duped her, and she has to suffer all alone, poor thing."

Rathamma had brought up Subbi from the days when she was a tiny tot and had developed an affection for Subbi's simple innocence.

But Venkayya was incapable of making any allowances, especially in matters like these. He got up from his cot a little irritated, not with Rathamma but with the situation itself. "Drive her out," he repeated.

"She ought to have thought twice before she allowed herself to be duped. How can she expect us now to keep her in the house as usual?" Rathamma got enraged against the male species, and the signs of irritation were prominent in her eyes. She raised her voice suddenly and said defiantly, "What can men understand about the difficulties of women? The fellow who spoils her walks about the streets like a prince, and this poor wretch has to put up with it all. God himself is partial to men. I cannot ask her to go away. You can knock her out yourself if you are so particular." She grew very excited, and Venkayya was utterly disarmed. He said indecisively, "What can we do then? She has brought it down upon herself." "Yes, but where is the harm if we keep her in the house? She is no relative of ours, and people cannot possibly find fault with us. It is a bit of generosity that we are showing, and generosity never goes without its reward. She has grown up under this roof, and therefore let her continue to be here." Venkayya did not say anything just then but walked out, frowning as if the whole business was muddled by the wife and rendered too difficult for him. Rathamma, of course, took it for granted that her husband's permission was as good as given for Subbi to continue to serve in the household. So Subbi continued to live with them, and she got on quite well indeed, with the unfailing attention of Rathamma on the one side compensating for the utter disgust of Venkayya on the other. Though Venkayya could not express himself strongly, he frequently lost his temper over trifles. This only resulted in Rathamma sticking to her resolution more strongly and in her taking even greater care of Subbi as if to shield the girl from the growing wrath of her husband. In short, Rathamma treated Subbi as if she were a daughter who had come from the husband's home to the mother' s for the confinement. Rathamma had faint recollections of all that preceded the birth of her one child, Jagannadha Rao. It was a unique experience for every woman. There would be a strong desire to eat special dishes, but nothing finally would please the palate. There would be moments when the whole world would seem loaded with despair. An extreme tenderness of spirit would be induced even in the wildest-tempered woman. Men too would regard a pregnant woman with more than ordinary tenderness. She would be conspicuous and would herself quite unconsciously assume an air of self-importance above all the people in the household. Though Subbi asked for nothing, Rathamma cooked for her a variety of puddings; and whether Subbi liked them or not, Rathamma derived the utmost satisfaction that she was performing the sacred duties of a mother towards this fallen woman.

In the course of time, Subbi gave birth to a male child. The child was very good-looking and plump. Rathamma's heart overflowed with pleasure when she saw the child, and she was tempted to take the child immediately in her arms, though she did not do so in fact. For twenty years now the rafters of this house had not heard the first shrill cry announcing the arrival of a new member of the species, and it did not matter to Rathamma whose child it was that now renewed the cry. In fact, she did not pause to think that the child was an illegitimate one, the fruit of an inexcusable breach of good conduct on the part of Subbi.

Rathamma tried to make Subbi confess at least at this stage who the father of this buxom baby was. But Subbi repeated the same old trick of weeping without a word.

One day Venkayya called his wife aside and said, "What has happened has happened. I think at least now we can send her away. The difficult time is over, and she can take care of herself now." "That is exactly why we need not," replied his wife. "We allowed her to give birth to the child under our roof. And now, why should we send her away? She will not repeat the mistake now that she knows what she has to put up with."

The child grew up in a shabby cradle on the verandah, and all his lullabies were from the crows in the daytime and the rats at night. The child was, however, perfectly satisfied with his surroundings and scarcely cried except when hungry. It was more than a surprise to Jagannadha Rao to find a baby of three months in the verandah when he came home for the next summer vacation. He approached his mother and asked her in a doubtful voice, "Whose child is it, mother?"

"Our Subbi's," replied his mother.

For the first time in his life, Jagannadha Rao realized that women, as a result of certain experiences, gave birth to children! "You know she is foolish," Rathamma went on, slicing the potato, "and some villain has done this mischief to her. And poor woman, she conceived. Father wanted to drive her out of the house, but I persisted in helping her. And she gave birth to this bright little thing in our own house."

She then began to generalize about the heartlessness of men and about the sympathy and generosity that women alone were capable of. But Jagannadha Rao understood not a word of it. The one fact that Subbi had become the mother of a child stood like a nightmare before him. The same evening, Rathamma was going to the well, carrying a brass vessel, and she had to cross the verandah. She saw two figures faintly, a little distance away, in the courtyard, and heard something like a murmur and a sob. She paused a little and listened attentively.

Don't weep. Here, take this rupee and buy something for the child. Why do you weep? I know it is my child. I will help you. Don't be afraid. You see, I....

She could easily recognize the voice of her son. And the two figures were Jagannadha Rao and Subbi! Involuntarily, she dropped the vessel to the ground. At the clink of the vessel, Jagannadha Rao and Subbi separated and disappeared.

Oh, what was this that had happened? She had never thought of this possibility! Her son! Her own dear son! How could he have done such a horrid thing? She had paid too dearly for bringing up a street wench in her house. The rogue! These wretches had no gratitude. It was Subbi that had seduced her son! She had all the while tended a venomous snake with her own hands. She never thought her own kindness would ultimately bring about this danger to her son. She once thought Subbi was foolish. But now she knew better! Subbi must have always known those vile tricks with which to dupe innocent young fellows like her son! What a fine pretence the jade kept up all the while! What horrid things these low-born women were capable of! She ran to her husband's room and broke out into a loud wail, as if the very foundations of the earth had been shaken.

"Everything is finished. You must come at once! All is lost! All is lost!

Venkayya came out, and Rathamma told him what she had overheard. Venkayya lost his balance of mind; he could not think sanely, but that was only for a moment.

He called for his son and for Subbi, but he could not extract anything at all from either of them, in spite of his assumed seriousness. Subbi continued to weep silently, and Jagannadha Rao kept silent with a frown on his forehead.

Venkayya then called his son into his room, made him sit down beside him, and cajolingly begged him to reveal the truth. For a long time Jagannadha Rao denied all knowledge of the affair, but when his father tenderly persisted and assured him that he need not fear any evil consequences, he nodded his head and accepted his role in the drama under review. Rathamma held her hands tightly against her temples. She felt disgusted with herself for the unbounded kindness she had shown Subbi while Subbi was pregnant. She had been rightly fooled. This wench knew everything but kept quiet, and she was misled about Subbi's real nature. Subbi had successfully played upon the innocence of her son. The wretch!

"Get out of this house," she roared. "Get out of my sight. We did not know that you were such a vile creature."

On the other hand, Venkayya was now sure that there could not be a more foolish creature than Subbi. The really clever ones, among whom his wife was classing Subbi, the street type, knew only too well how to deal with such a situation without letting it come to such a pass as having to give birth to an illegitimate child.

"Let her stay now, the poor girl," he said hesitatingly, "and we will think out afterwards what to do with her."

When he knew it was his own son that was responsible for the birth of this child, he was himself seized with a sense of moral responsibility and could not see the victim driven out without home or prospect.

But Rathamma was stubborn. She kept on saying, "No, she cannot remain any longer in my house, after what she has brought down upon us."

"She was only foolish, you know," pleaded Venkayya. "Let her stay for the night. We will send her away tomorrow. Where can she go in this darkness now?"

He remembered the days of his own youth. Though nothing of this sort had befallen him, he knew that it was merely luck, and he realized that nobody needed to be blamed in matters like this. People lost all foresight in the blinding instinct of the moment. His son was just as human as he was or as any other person that walked this globe. And Subbi was human too and not as wily as his wife now imagined her to be. But Rathamma broke into a fury. "You can build a palace for her if you like, but I cannot go on living under this roof with her. Either she or I must leave this house immediately. You can keep her if you are so particular. My word has never prevailed in this household, and what more can I expect now when both father and son are against me?" She was almost weeping, and Venkayya was again disarmed. He did not want to raise a family feud on account of a stupid little creature like Subbi, and so he said at last, addressing Subbi, "Go away to your grandmother's place." And he took out some money from his cash box and added, "Here, take these twenty rupees with you." He threw two ten-rupee notes in her direction, as if in disgust; but Rathamma snatched them away, saying, why these twenty rupees? She has already enjoyed much more than she deserves at our expense. We need not give her anything now."

Poor Subbi had to leave the house on that dark, chilly night with her child.

Venkayya did not sleep well that night. He kept thinking of poor Subbi and her ill-clothed baby. The next day he inquired about Subbi's whereabouts and went personally to a neighbouring village where she was reported to be and gave her, not just twenty rupees but a great deal more. And when Subbi started weeping, he not only assured her that he would look after Subbi's child as the child grew up but even promised to take Subbi back into service as soon as he could pacify the good old lady at home!

Translated by Shri Palagummi Padmaraju
(Rendered from the original story Subbi in Telugu)
Published in Triveni magazine- 1939

CHAPTER III

On The Boat

After Sundown the world was enveloped in a melancholy haze. The boat glided softly on the still river. The water lapped against the sides of the boat in soft ripples. No life stirred, as far as the eye could see, and the dead world hummed soundlessly. That hum was inaudible, but the body felt it, and it filled the mind with its reverberations. A feeling of life coming to an end, of peace inexorable and devoid of all hope, crept over one's consciousness. The vague, mysterious figures of distant trees moved along with the boat motionlessly. The trees, which were nearer, moved backwards, like devils with dishevelled hair. The boat did not move. The canal bank moved backwards. My eyes looked deep into the still waters, penetrating the darkness. The stars relaxed on the bed of water, swinging dreamily on the slow ripples, and slept with eyes wide open. No stir in the air. The rope by which the boatmen pulled the boat sagged and tautened rhythmically, and the bells on the guide stick in the hand of the leader tinkled at each step. At one end of the boat, there was the red glare of a fire in the oven, alternately glowing into a flame and subsiding. With a small bucket, a boy bailed out the water percolating into the boat through small leaks. Sacks filled with paddy, jaggery, tamarind, and whatnot were stacked in the boat. I lay down on the top of the boat, staring at the sky. From inside the boat, tobacco smoke, mingled with soft, inaudible voices, spread in all directions. In the small room where the clerk sat, there was a tiny oil lamp, blinking in the darkness. The boat moved on. A voice hailed us from the distance, "Please bring the boat to this bank – this bank!" As the boat drew near the bank, two figures jumped on the footboard. The boat tilted slightly to that side. "Please do not mind us. We'll sit here on the top," said a woman's voice.

The man at the rudder asked her, "Where were you all these days, Rangi? I have not seen you for a long time." "My man took me to many places – Vijayanagaram and Visakhapatnam – and we climbed together the Hill of Apanna." "Where are you going now?"

"Mandapaka. How are you, brother? Do you still have the same clerk?"

"Yes."

The male figure fell down in a heap, and his lighted cheroot slipped from his mouth. The woman put it out.

"Sit down properly," she said.

"Shut up, you bitch. Do you think I am drunk? I'll break your ribs if you disturb me."

He rolled over from one side to the other. The woman covered him with the sheet of cloth which had slipped to one side when he rolled over. She lighted a cheroot herself. When the match caught the flame, I saw her face for a brief moment. The dark face glowed red. There was a hint of a bass in her voice. When she talked, you felt she was artlessly confiding to you her innermost secrets. She was not beautiful; her hair was dishevelled. And yet there was an air of dignity about her. The black blouse she was wearing gave the impression that she was not wearing anything. In the darkness her eyes sparkled as if they were very much alive.

When she lighted the match, she noticed me lying nearby. "There is someone sleeping here," she said, trying to wake up the man.

"Lie down, you slut. I'll break your neck if you disturb me again."

With an effort he moved away from me. The clerk stood on the footboard with the oil lamp in his hand. He asked, "Who is that fellow, Rangi?" "He is my man, Paddalu. Please do not charge us, sir, for the journey."

"Is it Paddalu? Get him out! He is a rogue and a thief. Have you no sense? He's dead drunk, and you have brought him onto this boat!"

"Who says I am drunk?" complained Paddalu.

"You fools, throw the fellow out. Why did you allow him to step on the boat? He is dead drunk," the clerk shouted to the boatmen.

"I'm not dead drunk. I merely quenched a little of my thirst," protested Paddalu. "Why don't you keep mum?" admonished the woman. "Please, sir, I beg of you. May God bless you, sir. We'll get down at Mandapaka," she pleaded. The man joined in the pleading, "I'm not drunk, sir. Please be kind and allow us to go to Mandapaka." "If you make any row, I'll have you thrown into the canal. Be careful." The clerk went back to his room. Paddalu sat up. He was not really drunk. "He will have me thrown into the canal – the son of a bitch!" he said in a low voice. "Keep quiet. If he heard what you said, then we're finished." "Let him look around the boat tomorrow morning. He puts on airs, the son of a bitch."

"S... s...s... Someone is sleeping there."

Paddalu lighted a cheroot. He had a very thick moustache. His face was oval. His spine curved like a bow drawn by a string. He was lean and sinewy, and there was an air of nonchalance about him. The boat was gliding along softly again. The boatmen were washing the utensils after food, talking among themselves. It was not cool, but I covered myself with a sheet. I felt a little afraid to leave my body exposed helplessly to the darkness. The breeze was sharp – the boat glided softly on the water like the touch of a woman. The night was wrapped with tenderness – as in the caress of an unseen woman. I felt lost in that embrace, and many memories of my past and of tales tinged with melancholy about a woman tending a man and bringing him happiness flitted across my consciousness. At a little distance from me, two cheroots were glowing red in the darkness. It appeared as though life was sitting there heavily, smoking, and thinking about itself.

"Which is the next village on our way?" asked Paddalu.

"Kaldari", said Rangi.

"We have a long distance to go."

"Don't do it today. You ought to be careful. Not today. We will try some other time when it is safer. Will you not listen to me?" pleaded Rangi.

"You are afraid – you slut," said Paddalu. He tickled her side with a dig of his finger.

"Oh!" she said and looked skyward as if she wished the feeling this would last forever.

Gradually I fell asleep. The boat moved downstream as if also in sleep. The two figures not far from me were talking in whispers to each other for some time. Though I was sleeping, a part of me was awake. I knew that the boat was moving, that the water was lapping its sides, and that the trees on the banks were moving backwards. Inside the boat everyone was asleep; Rangi moved from my side to the rudder and sat beside the man who was handling it. "How are you, brother?" she asked.

"How are you?" asked the man at the rudder. "Oh! What wonders we have seen, my man and I!

We went to a cinema. We saw a ship. What a ship it was! Brother, it was as big as our village. I do not know where its rudder was." She told him of a hundred things, and her voice caressed me in my sleep. "Oh girl! I am feeling sleepy," said the man at the rudder. "I'll hold it; you lie down there," said Rangi. The boat moved on silently and slowly. Without disturbing the silence, Rangi raised her voice into a song:

Where is he? Oh, where is he, my man! I put the food on the plate and

Sit there awaiting his return.

Like a shadow the night deepens.

But no sleep comes to my eyes. Where is he? My man? The cold wind stings me like a scorpion.

And my nerves contract and ache, Unless you press me with your warm body, I may die. Where is he? - My man!

Rangi's voice had music in it. It seemed as though all living creatures heard the song in their sleep. Age-old tales of love reverberated sadly and mysteriously in that song. It spread like a sheet of water, and the world was afloat in it like a small boat. Human life, with its love and longing, seemed heavy, inevitable, and strange. A little distance from me, Paddalu sat with his head covered with a sheet. But a gulf seemed to separate him from Rangi. After some time Paddalu went inside the boat. I shook off sleep and lay looking at the stars. Rangi was singing:

You thought there was a girl in the lane behind the hut.

And sneaked there silently. But who is the girl, my dear man? Is she not I in my bloom...?

Rangi's song travelled through the worlds and then returned and touched me somewhere in my heart. I felt drowsy. In my sleep, the elemental longing of man and woman for one another danced before me like rustic lovers playing hide and seek. A dream world, entirely new to me, spread before me in my sleep. Rangi and Paddalu moved about in a myriad of forms. The song slipped away from my consciousness, and the doors of my mind were gradually closed even to dreams. Some confusion in the boat woke me, and I sat up. The boat was tied to a peg on the bank. The boatmen were moving about hurriedly in the boat and on the bank with lanterns. On the bank, two men stood on either side of Rangi, holding her by her arms. One of them was the clerk. He had a piece of rope folded in one of his hands. It looked as if Rangi was going to receive a thrashing. I jumped onto the bank and asked them what was wrong. The clerk's face flushed with anger. He said, "The rogue has run away with some of our things. This daughter of a bitch must have got the boat to a bank while everybody was asleep. She was holding the rudder, the slut." There was a note of despair and helplessness in his tone. "What were the goods that were stolen?" I asked.

"Two baskets of jaggery and three bags of tamarind. That was why I said I would not allow them on the boat. I will have to make up the loss." Then he asked Rangi, "Where did he unload the goods?"

"Near Kaldari, my good sir!"

"You liar! All of us were awake at Kaldari." "Then it must have been at Nidadavolu."

"No, she will never tell us. We will hand her over to the police at Attili. Get on the boat."

"Kind sir, please allow me to go."

"Get on the boat," he ordered, pushing her towards the boat.

Two boatmen dragged her into the boat.

"Sleepy beggars! Careless idiots! Have you no sense of responsibility? Why should you put the rudder in her hands?" The clerk was very much put out. He went back to his room. Rangi resumed her former seat. One boatman sat beside her to guard her.

The boat moved again. I lighted a cheroot.

"Kind sir, spare me one too," she asked me in a tone which suggested intimacy. I gave her a cheroot and a box of matches. She lighted it. "Dear brother! What can you gain by handing me over to the police?"

"The clerk will not let you go," said the boatman.

"Is Paddalu your husband?" I asked her. "He is my man," she replied.

The boatman said, "He seduced her when she was a young girl. He did not marry her. Now he has another girl. Where is she, Rangi?"

"In Kovvur. Now, she is in her bloom. When she has endured as many blows as I have, she will look worse than me. The dirty bitch!"

"Then why do you have anything to do with him?" I asked. "He is mine, sir!" she replied, as if that explained everything.

"But he has another woman."

"What can he do without me? It does not matter how many women a man has. I tell you, sir; he is a king among men. There is not another like him."

The boatman said, "Sir, you cannot imagine what this fellow really is without knowing him. She was just bubbling with life and youth when she got entangled with him. One night, he locked her up in her hut and set fire to it. She was almost burnt to death. It was only her good fortune that saved her." "I felt like strangling him with my bare hands if I could only get at him. A red-hot bamboo fell across my back from the roof of the hut." She lifted her blouse a little, and even in that darkness I could see a white scar on her back. "Why are you still with him after all this cruelty?" I asked. "I cannot help it, sir. When he is with me, I simply cling to him. He can talk so well, and your sense of pity wells up like a spring. This evening we started from Kovvur. On the way, he begged me on his knees to help him in this affair. He said he was completely broke. We reached the Nidadavolu channel by a shortcut across the fields...

"Where did he land the goods?" "How should I know?"

"Oh! She will never tell the truth, the rogue!" said the boatman laughing.

There was a sudden impulse of curiosity in me to have a close look at her face. But in that darkness, she remained hazy and inscrutable. The boat crawled slowly on the smooth sheet of water. As midnight passed, the breeze developed a colder sting. There was a slight rustle of leaves on the trees. I did not sleep again that night. Rangi's guard tried ineffectually to fight his overpowering desire to sleep and finally yielded to it. But Rangi sat there listlessly smoking her cheroot, reconciled to her position. "You were not married at all?" I asked her.

"No. I was very young when Paddalu took me away."
"Which is your native village?"

"Indrapalem... Then I did not know he was a drunkard. Now, of course, I have caught it from him. There is nothing wrong if one drinks. But sometimes when he is drunk, he is wild."

"You could have left him and gone back to your parents." "That is what I feel like when he becomes wild. But then there is no one else like him. You do not know him. When he is not drunk, he is as meek as a lamb. He might take a hundred women. But he comes back to me. What can he do without me?"

The woman's attitude struck me as strange, and I could not derive what held those two together. Rangi said again, "No job suited either of us. So, we had to take to thieving. When my mother was alive, she used to scold me for making a fool of myself. One night, he brought that girl to my hut." "Which girl?" "The one he is now living with. He put her on my bed and lay down beside her. Before my very eyes! Both of them were drunk. The slut! I pounced upon her and scratched her violently. He intervened and beat me out of my breath. At about midnight, he went away with her somewhere. He returned again. I called him names and refused to admit him into the house. He collapsed on the doorstep and began to weep like a child. I was touched. I sat beside him. He took me into his lap and asked me to give him my necklace. 'What for?' I asked him. He said it was for the other girl. I was beside myself with anger and heaped on him torments of abuse. He told me, weeping, that he could not live without that girl. My anger knew no bounds. I pushed him out and bolted the door inside. He pulled at it for a while and went away. I lay with my eyes wide open and could not sleep for a long time. But after I fell asleep, the house caught fire. He had locked the hut on the outside and set fire to it. I tried the door desperately, and at that time of the night, my shouts for help did not reach my neighbours. My body was being fried alive. I fell unconscious. My neighbours must have rescued me in that state. The police arrested him the next day. But I told them categorically that he could not have been the author of the crime. That evening he came to me and wept for hours. Sometimes, when he is drunk, he weeps like that. But when he is not drunk, he is such a jolly fellow. I gave him that necklace." "Why do you still assist him in these crimes?"

"What am I to do when he comes and begs me as if his whole life depends on it?"

"Did he really take you to all those places, Vijayanagar, Visakhapatnam and whatnot?"

"No. I wanted to gain the confidence of the boatmen. On two former occasions, this very boat was robbed." "What will you do if the police arrest you?"

"Why should I do anything? What can they do? I have no stolen goods in my possession. Who knows who was responsible for the robbery? They might beat me. But ultimately they will have to set me free."

"Supposing Paddalu is caught with these goods?"

"No, he would have disposed of them by now. I remained in the boat to give him enough time to effect his escape." She heaved a sigh and then said, in a soft voice, "All this goes to that damned bitch. He will not leave her till her freshness fades away. I have to suffer all this for the sake of that slut." There was not a trace of emotion in her voice, nor was there any reproach. She accepted him as he was and was prepared to do anything for him. It was not sacrifice, not devotion, not even love. It was simply the heart of a woman, with a strange complex of feelings, tinged with love as well as with jealousy. There was only one outward expression of this medley of feelings, and that was the longing she felt for her man. Every fibre of that heart thirsted for that man. But she had no demands to make of him, ethical or moral. She did not mind if he was not true to her, even if he was cruel to her. She loved him as he was, with all his vagaries and pettiness's and with his wild and untamed spirit. What did she derive from such a life with the dice so loaded against her? What was her compensation? Was not such a life very unhappy and burdensome? But then what was happiness except the lack of a consciousness of unhappiness? Was I happy judging by that standard?

The wind rose gradually. The boat moved faster. There were signs of the world waking up slowly from its rejuvenating slumber. Here and there peasants could be seen going to their fields. The morning star had not yet risen. Rangi drew her knees closer, folded her arms around them, and sat looking into the fading night. "He is my man. Wherever he goes, he is bound to return to me," she said slowly, not particularly addressing me. These words summarised the one hope, the one strength, and the one faith that kept her irrevocably linked with life. Her whole life revolved around that one point. There was pity, fear, and above all, reverence in my heart for that woman. I wondered how confusing, grotesque, terrifying, and even insane the affairs of the human heart were! I sat looking at her till the day broke. Before I got off the boat, I put a rupee in her hand without being observed and then went away without waiting to see her reaction. I never met her again.

Translated by Shri Palagummi Padmaraju
(Rendered from the original story Padava Prayanam in Telugu)
Published in Sahitya Akademi - 1959

Trivia: -

The short story: On the Boat, was made into a movie named "Stri" released in 1995 and was directed by the veteran Film maker shri K. Sethumadhavan. The film garnered two National Film Awards and two Nandi Awards and was showcased in the Indian Panorama section of the International Film Festival of India and the 2nd Prague International Film Festival.

National Film Award for Best Feature Film in Telugu – 1995

National Film Award – Special Mention – Actress Rohini!

CHAPTER IV

Coolies

Any day now, water would be let into the canal. Still, a hundred yards of the canal had to be deepened, and the breaches in the banks filled up to contain the fresh inflow of water. If I failed to accomplish the task before the water was let in, the authorities would hold up the bills of the contractor, and he would take it out on me, the poor clerk. I gathered as many coolies as I could during the night.

The dried-up canal was thirsting for water. On either bank, clusters of mangoes were hanging from the trees, pulling down the branches by their weight. The sun had not yet risen, and already the promise of unbearable heat was in the air. Except for a little water that had oozed into the temporary pool dug in the sandy bed of the canal, the landscape was waterless as far as the eye could see. But the trees were deep green.

Through the gaps in the clouds of the eastern sky, the sun rose big and red. The village was on the western bank of the canal. I sat on the canal bank anxiously and desperately urging the coolies on. Despite my exhortations, the coolies kept to their slow pace of work. Slowly they filled the cane baskets with earth. The women coolies leisurely lifted the baskets onto their heads and emptied the earth into the breaches in the canal banks. The sun was growing intense with every minute. The sun makes everything lethargic. Air hangs motionless. But the earth drinks in the sun and breaks into chunks, regaining its fertility. The sun gives the earth a great capacity for thirst.

The earth learns to drink up whole torrents of rain in the season and yields crops in profusion for another year. Sweat glistened on the Black bodies of the coolies. It gave a strange lustre to their hard muscles. Men and women worked and talked incessantly. The laziest of them all was the big fellow with the bushy moustaches. His name was Sathireddy. He had a sharp wit, and the coolies forgot to work, listening to him. He would plunge his crowbar into the earth once in a while and take his own time over a funny anecdote. But he was strong as an ox. An eighteen-year-old girl filled her basket with lumps of earth he dug. She stood for a while listening to him. Then she lifted the basket on to her head and walked away. Her name was Rathi. Her place was taken by a woman of thirty. She threw the basket down and took the cheroot out of her mouth. The woman-coolies smoke their cheroots, keeping the lighted ends inside their mouths. They call it 'short-cut smoke'. She cleared the ash with her little finger, drew on it till the lighted end glowed red and put it again inside her mouth. She was Chellamma. "Fill up, girl, and don't stand looking," said Sathireddy. "You poke," she said between her teeth on account of the cheroot. He laughed at the vulgarism, and she smiled.

The sun was getting hotter every moment. The voices of the coolies sounded like a distant hum. Eighteen-year-old Rathi suddenly broke into a screeching laugh. Her husband was digging with abandon a little distance away. His movements had the slow grace of an animal. He was throwing ribald songs in the faces of the woman coolies who came to him. His name was Musaliah. There was an old man by the name of Paddalu who was about fifty; he was a Harijan by caste, and he was describing the miraculous power of his village deity, Mavullamma. Morning was ripening into noon. I got up from the canal bank and sat in the shelter of the front veranda of the Karanam's house. The house was abutting the canal bank. In a corner of the thatched roof hung a cluster of paddy stalks full of grain. Sparrows hanging obliquely onto the stalks pecked at the grain. On the closed half of the 'pial', paddy was stocked in a granary improvised with thick ropes of hay and plastered on the outside with mud. The other side of the 'pial' opened into a neat level yard. Vapours rising from the earth gave the landscape a fluid appearance. The slow sun hurt the eyes. Under the shade of the tamarind tree in the front yard, a cow chewed the cud, standing drowsily. Old Paddalu was narrating: "On the day of the festival, they sacrifice a he-buffalo. A heavy sword is used for the purpose. The head must be severed with one stroke. If it does not, it bodes evil. The blood is caught in a big earthenware dish. It is put near the feet of the deity. The temple door is closed. Five locks are put on the door by the heads of the five surrounding villages. The Karanams and Munsiffs of the five villages put seals on the locks. Throughout the night, washermen keep vigil around the temple. Early the next morning, the seals and the locks are checked, and the temple door is opened. Not a drop of blood will be left in the dish. The deity leaves a few things in the dish which signify her prophecies for the year. Water indicates plenty of rain. Cotton threads mean that cloth will be cheaper. Every prophecy comes true..." Young Musaliah untied the cloth round his waist and wore it round his head as protection against the sun. He tucked up the loose ends of his dhoti behind him, taking them between his legs. Sathireddy took time lighting his cheroot and resumed his work.

Work slowed down. The lifted crowbars sank into the earth, tired and out of control. The sun was reaching the top of the head. The village looked parched in the sun. Crows jumped open-mouthed from branch to branch. Then Sathireddy plunged his crowbar into the earth and did not lift it up again. They all threw away their implements. The work was halfway through. It could be completed if the canal remained closed till the evening. Sathireddy was washing himself near the well on the bank. Rathi asked him for some water. He drew a bucketful from the well, but before giving the bucket to her, he threw a handful of water on her face. "You rogue," she shouted in mock anger.

Rathi's husband looked daggers at them. Sathireddy tasted the water and spat it out, making a wry face. "Phew, it's saltish," he cried.

All the coolies ran to the freshwater pool in the bed of the canal. The water got dirty in a minute. Paddalu admonished them, though he was of a lower caste. "See what you have done. Where can we get water to drink after finishing our food? You have churned up the little good water we have. Everyone agreed that Paddalu was right, but the mischief was done, Musaliah said. "By the time we finish eating, the water will be clear." There was hunger in the hollowness of his voice. He was a toddy tapper by caste, and there was in his bearing a headlong recklessness characteristic of that caste. He looked as though he would swing his fist at someone even without any provocation. He and Rathi were eating out of the same vessel, rice soaked in Gangi (a kind of gruel) with salt and fried prawns. Sathireddy distributed small bits of pickle he had brought to everyone. He gave a particularly large bit to Rathi. Chellamma smiled, indicating that she had observed his partiality. The smile was tinged with a little jealousy. Musaliah looked at Chellamma and Rathi. Rathi laughed awkwardly. The trees looked up at the sky, tired and weak. The world had the pitiful look of a criminal condemned to eternal punishment. But the tender leaves on the edges of the branches were hardening into green. Beds of paddy seedlings looked like green carpets spread here and there to relieve the monotony of the long stretch of dark brown earth. The slow, unquenchable thirst in the air made all living things drowsy. The crows shifted their one-eyed looks this way and that in search of the non-existent coolness. Their beaks were permanently open, making silent sounds. I spread a mat on the 'pial' and lay down, looking at the roof sightlessly. The coolies washed their vessels after eating their food. They dipped their vessels into the pool of fresh water without disturbing it and drank their fill. They gathered around the trunk of the tamarind tree and pulled out tobacco from inside the folds of their turbans. They wetted the leaves and rolled them into cheroots. I did not notice when the sun started its descent. I woke up suddenly from a kind of drugged daydream and began urging the coolies to start work again. They got up unhurried and complacent, winding the turbans round their heads. The women coolies tied cloth rings over their heads to seat the baskets of earth. Without bending, they kicked up the edges of their baskets with their left feet and caught the rising edges dexterously with their left hands. The men tucked up the loose ends of their dhotis behind them, drawing them between their legs.

They drew the last puffs on their cheroots greedily before throwing them away. The work gathered momentum rather too slowly for my liking. Sathireddy started singing just to take his mind away from the sweltering heat. Why do you giggle, oh girl?

Looking at me?

And wipe the sweat on your cheek and throw it at me?

Near the hut in the lane at dusk

There'll be none.

Why do you exhibit your eagerness? In this broad daylight?

Musaliah took up from there and sang a variety of songs. They struck a layer of sand beneath the black earth. So, they laid aside their crowbars and took up spades. Rathi kept the basket slantwise with her left knee, and Sathireddy filled it up with spadefuls of sand. Playfully, he swung a spadeful of sand on to the bare midriff of Rathi. In mock disgust she kicked away the basket of sand on to his thighs, pretending to be annoyed. She dusted her navel and legs, abusing Sathireddy. Musaliah stopped singing and looked at her. The sun was descending. The air cooled a little. The work gathered momentum as it reached its final stages. My mind was free from anxiety. I sat on the bank watching the coolies respectfully. Their concentration was divine. Once they got into stride, there was no stopping them. But you could not hurry them, however much you tried. Their sense of urgency was on a different scale. They had their own estimate of time and work, and they knew they could finish a job in a certain duration. Once we entrusted a job to them, we were in their hands. Our anxiety should await their pleasure. In a way we were their slaves. Suddenly Musaliah threw a basket at Rathi with devilish force. Terror capered in Rathi's face and eyes. He lifted the basket again and hit her on the head. She lifted her hands in defence, covering her face with them. The end of her saree slipped from her shoulder and breasts. Blood trickled down from her nose and lips. The men threw their implements and ran to hold Musaliah. Rathi wailed helplessly, shivering like a leaf in a storm. "You dirty bitch!" was all that Musaliah could blurt out, choked with anger. He was in the grip of an uncontrollable rage.

Paddalu tried to calm him down.

"Shame on you; you exhibit your strength on that chip of a girl," he said.

I hurried to the spot and enquired as to the cause of the outburst. Shaking in every limb and throwing his words in a stutter, Musaliah said.

"She is flirting, the slut."

"No, sir, on my oath, I didn't do anything," pleaded Rathi pathetically. She looked around as though she were appealing for the protection of her life.

"Shut up, you jade," shouted Musaliah, "I'll skin you alive."

He threw away the men holding him in a giant heave and ran towards Rathi, who forgot even to run away, petrified with fear. Before he could get hold of her hair, Sathireddy deftly caught him from behind in his vice-like grip and held him fast. He said in a cool voice.

"Cool down, brother. Why kick up such a row over an innocent joke?"

Sathireddy released him when he was certain that he had cooled down sufficiently. Then he exhorted the coolies. "Take up your spades. Come along, girls, with your baskets. It's already sundown, and we have a lot of work on hand." They resumed their work again. But the painful beating of my heart against my ribs did not subside for a long while. I sat looking at Musaliah apprehensively. The last breach in the canal bank was filled up as the sun sank behind the western horizon. The moon, which had come up sometime during the afternoon, was warm. One or two of the more thrifty coolies, who had saved a spot of their midday meal for the evening, ate it. I sat watching Musaliah and Rathi, apprehending an outburst at any moment. Some of them asked me for some money. I made a part payment, telling them that the final settlement would be made on the following day. They went away in a bustle, and Musaliah and Rathi were among them. I dined at the Karanam's house that night. They gave me a cot, and I put it in the open yard on the southern side of the 'pial'. The moon was at the apex of the sky, shedding warm blue light. I lay down thinking of Musaliah and Rathi; I could not get them out of my mind. The untamed wild animal in him and the helpless fragility in her disturbed me. I was afraid that something terrible was going to happen that night. I had heard of many instances of murder among rural folk for ostensibly lesser reasons. As I was slipping into a doze, I heard them coming back, evidently from the toddy shop, in high spirits.

Men and women were pushing and cursing each other, laughing rather loudly. They threw themselves down, anywhere anyhow, some on the bank and some on the sandy bed of the canal; Musaliah and Rathi appeared to have had a drop more than the others. They walked unsteadily to the shade of the tamarind tree and literally collapsed near the trunk. Sathireddy, rolling on the grassy patch beside the well, sang, lifting his voice rather high; the effigy of fortune capered on the tamarind bough.

The wayside goddess, Musalamma, had gone for her confinement...

Many other voices took up the chorus, "For her confinement," words rolling heavily on their drunken tongues. Voices rose all out of tune. The whole effect was eerie. Sathireddy sang, Let's sacrifice a couple of he-buffalos to Potharaju and migrate to another place...'

Then Musaliah found his voice.

The buxom lass raised her hands working the ware-lift, and her blouse protested with a tearing sound p-r-r-r. Soon, the songs got mixed up, several singers raising their voices at once, in a variety of keys. Gradually, the voices sounded thin and drowsy, and then I did not hear them anymore. My mind was hazy with sleep. But I was conscious of the cool touch of the moon. Suddenly I felt some movement beside my cot. I opened my eyes and looked without moving. About ten yards away, I saw two figures locked in a half embrace, walking unsteadily. I recognised them as Musalia and Rathi. He whispered hoarsely in her ears; Let's get on to the pial."

"In this broad moonlight?" asked Rathi.

"Get along, you slut," gurgled Musaliah, entwining his hands around her waist from behind. She laughed in her throat, leaning back on him. He lifted her bodily and carried her on to the pial, while she giggled happily. I was puzzled, but my mind was at peace.

Some confusion woke me up. I sat up on my cot, rubbing my eyes. I saw some coolies hurriedly throwing baskets, crowbars, and spades on to the bank. Some were left on the bed of the canal after work the previous evening. Then I saw the wet streak shining in the darkness at the bottom of the canal. The canal was opened, and it would be full by the morning. The moon had already set. I looked at the 'pial'; it was dark there – too dark. But I knew that all was well. I felt a sort of fulfilment brimming in my heart. I slept without a care in the world till the hard sun tickled my eyes.

Translated by Shri.Palagummi Padmaraju.
(Rendered from the original story Coolie Janam in Telugu)
Published by Sahitya Akademi – 1980

CHAPTER V

Viyyanna Grandfather's Demise

No one ever thought that our Viyyanna thatha would die like this at last. Whatever he does, he never does it like all the others. But he died like all the others. By the time Grandfather died, our real grandfather was missing from him. Or he died a few hours before that. In fact, we all firmly believed that our thatha would never die like this. Rathi, the toddy tapper woman who is Thatha's keep, got up early that morning and went to the fields for milking the cows. By the time she came back, it was nearing seven o'clock. As there were no signs of thatha having gotten up, she pushed the door and entered, vexed. At the same time, I was walking towards the canal bund to answer nature's call. From inside, Rathi's angry voice was audible. 'Get up! What sleep? It's already late.

'The same every day, still asleep....'

Rathi's voice changed. 'Thatha! Thatha! Tha...' She made a sound that had never been heard before. Pushing the door, I also entered. Rathi went blank on seeing me. "Tha... tha!"

Rathi did not cry, but she did as much! In fact, Rathi never cries. She never laughed and never cried either. Even in very happy situations, she never laughed. Even when very important people passed away, she did not weep. That does not mean either that our thatha is not a very important person, and Rathi has no such love lost for thatha. Since I said that, a grandfather, you must have all got confused. If it comes to that, he is a grandfather for everyone. Whoever imagines a thatha in their own way, thatha appears like that to them. He is a definition for the class of thathas or grandfathers. Everyone knows him only as a thatha. No one knows what other name one should address him by. Even Rathi used to call him thatha.

In fact, it is fifteen years since our thatha started dying. He kept on dying at least once a year. But in order to die again the next year, he kept living. And all the villagers were disgusted that he would never die. This time, however, he died not to live again. Viyyanna thatha, however much he did not believe in living, had never believed in death either. No one knows anything about death. About living, everyone knows a bit or more. So instead of dying the unknown death, it's better to live the known life, was his argument. If death is better, why doesn't all this world die all at once? It was only a few days back that all our villagers started considering him a dangerous man. Usually elders in the villages would keep women. Even if all those who maintain keeps are not gentlemen, all gentlemen would have keeps. It's a kind of status indication.

But in our village, one gentleman never had a keep. Though he was not highly educated, since all his relatives in other places were all well-educated, he would know the worldly things much better than all the others. He would read the newspaper daily and comment for the benefit of village elders. Since he never had a keep, all the village elders accepted his specialty. About the inner purport of the rituals like widow remarriage—though he never got his widowed daughter married again—now and then he would explain in his lectures. About many other things, he would discuss and explain. Even with knowledge of all such things, the fact that he let his daughter remain a widow was the reason for the respect the entire village had for him.

There is another reason that there could be liberty to a certain extent in man-woman relations, that it is not a sin to keep a keep; however much sacrosanct marriage is, it would not get despoiled just like that, he averred. With that, all those village elders, who consider it a sinful act and then could not put a stop to the habit, were consoled and felt comfortable. In spite of all the knowledge, since he never kept a woman, all of them venerated him with a lot of respect and devotion.

One day he came to our thatha's home and invited him for lunch to his place. It was the first ever time any fellow Brahmin invited thatha over for lunch. thatha felt a little funny. 'Why?' he asked demandingly.

'Nothing! It's my father's anniversary. I did not like you being separated from among us like this.... I have been thinking of inviting you for a long time.

'Then why did you stop?'

The gentleman cleared his throat and spoke mildly.

'I don't worry about such things. Each for his own likes and dislikes. Each for his habits. Just because of that ...' he did not know what to say for that.

'Listen to me. You came to me to invite me as if doing a favour. Talking of habits, I shall tell you. I am not habituated to visiting other people's places. You are talking about Rathi....'

'Never! Thatha garu! Never that. I don't care for such things. I respect you for your courage. What? Is it a big mistake'?

'If it is not a mistake, why did you not go for a keep? Don't go about prancing before me. I go according to my wish. Am I worried about your approval whether it is a big mistake or not'?

Terrified, the gentleman who came departed. There are many people who have keeps. But usually, they don't go about it openly. It was very usual to act as if they knew nothing even if the matter was known to all and sundry.

Against this usual, Viyyanna thatha openly keeping Rathi right at home was not slipping down the gullets for people to talk boldly about the matter was also equally difficult. So, they started considering him a dangerous man. Parents with children had to eschew visits to his place.

Of the real death of Viyyanna thatha, one must listen only while he narrates. But he did not really die at that time. 'Okay! In fact, I am a man like a peacock, he would once in a while tell. But that's a simple bluff. The debauchery is not just one of his habits. He never set foot in Bogam Street. Even then there was intensity in him. Instances of his life have to be thought about separately from one another. One such is the first touch of Rathi. Rathi has a lot of history behind him. She and her brother are orphans. The trials of marriage did not take place in time when she came of age. Though she was silent, stubborn, and unapproachable by habit, age has established its trickery. A well-built toddy tapper friend was on his way to Rangoon, and she looked at him peculiarly and threw a smile. Smiling, she also went to Rangoon along. But after a few months, the youth was not to be found, even after searching; she came back home with six months of pregnancy. Brother thrashed her. She did not cry. She did not revolt. Her brother administered her a medicine obtained from someone. Pregnancy fell off, but she remained outside the hut for four days, struggling for life. Then she sustained herself and got up. She thought all that as a natural phenomenon. She did not utter a word about anyone. But she would raise her voice sky-high and would almost beat up the youth who dared to leer at her. She has never cried since that day. Never laughed. She never looked at any male and threw that smile.

Later Rathi joined as a housemaid in our Viyyanna, that's homestead. Gradually she recovered and her breasts shining better than the days of going to Rangoon. Her hands grew smoother than that day. But the sage could not ascertain its trickery. She was like a ripe lime fruit. But if you look at her face, there would be a thorn ready to take a bite. Those were the days when Viyyannathatha's wife and son were alive. Naturally peacock-like, our Viyyanna thatha, one day when she was sweeping the floor, looked at her in a way. She roared. Though a bit afraid, mustering courage, he went near and with a voice dying in his throat said, 'Rathi.' She raised her hand high and slapped him hard. That evening on, she stopped coming to work. Later, for some time, Viyyanna thatha forgot about Rathi. Though there was another maid in

Rathi's place, Viyyanna, that never took a slap on the cheek from her.

Cholera came to our village. O.K., it came to Viyyanna thatha also. One day he lost consciousness. Before he returned to consciousness, the cholera outbreak that caused the son to die was all over. He realized gradually his resurrection from death first and then also the failure of the son's recovery. But then he did not feel any anger, nor sorrow. Simply felt hungry. In spite of that, the doctor never allowed food for four more days. On the first day his hunger was satiated, he wept because it would not be normal not to. 'Why was it not me to die?' he cried. But somehow, he felt a little satisfied that he was not dead himself. A score of days passed. All were thinking that cholera was going away from the village. Maybe it thought why it should leave, like all of them were thinking, cholera.

Baby returned suddenly and caught hold of thatha's wife. After four days, by the fifth evening, it appeared to be on the decline. By that time, Viyyanna thatha was well recovered. Cooking and all that at home, he was struggling about himself. Vexing, he would even give water and other things to the wife when she demanded. To the eyes that toiled for four days, a little stupor came about. In his dream, his son laughed with all his teeth exposed. 'Wait, you fool!' he wanted to say but hesitated. The Vimanam departed to the roof, and the boy looked back at him, the sky breaking open and bringing a stream along with fish huge as whales falling on the earth; from out of it, a king and his minister got down with glittering attires and many more things appeared to him. Meanwhile, a rumbling of devil's fight was heard, and Viyyanna thatha woke up suddenly. The lamp was gone; he went to the cot. The cot was mumbling. He shook the patient, and when he called, she simply said, 'Ummmm' and started mumbling again. 'What's all this funny act?' thought Viyyanna thatha. Not knowing which way the door is, he squatted next to the cot. The cot shook a little. He shuddered and laid his hand on the patient. The patient was shivering hard. He removed the hand with a jerk. The rumbling ceased. The rattling sound of insects raised a scale. Something in the darkness was turning into knots. What's all this? thought Viyyanna thatha. Meanwhile, something stopped suddenly. That was patent's shivering. He called out mildly. No answer came. Doubting what danger would come about, he could not call out loud. Snoring was heard softly. Like the saw cutting jerkily, Viyyanna thatha's heart became cold. Struggling like one drowning in water for a while, he opened the doors and came out at last. He shuddered like someone was chasing him. Leaving the village, he proceeded towards the fields.

He walked, trying to split the headache open and pull the ideas out. Fields, trees, and all were pitch dark. He walked along the field bunds without a direction. Trees appeared like village goddesses with their hair spread wide around. Water in the stream glows once in a while like a snake slithering. Here and there, cattle lying lazily were ruminating in sleep. From atop a toddy tree, sap was dripping from the slit bunch since the opening of the pot was not in place. A drop fell, sweet and fresh, on Viyyanna Thatha's face. 'Thu...' he said. 'Who's that?' called out a woman's voice.

'Thu!' said thatha again.

'Why don't you speak? Who's that?'

Aside on the elevated piece of land there was a sound of a grassy bed. Somebody getting up and adjusting the saree was coming near.

'Why?' Said Viyyanna thatha," 'I am asking who that is.'

'It's me.'

'Who? Is it thathagaru?'

But Viyyanna thatha could not identify the female voice. Like an injured bird, he fell to the ground and squatted. She eagerly came near and held him, saying, 'Ayya!' The leg slipped; leave me; it's all right. To look at the living being getting up from amidst the darkness, that he felt irritated. Her touch was unwanted by him. He thought of avoiding it immediately. He could not come up with equal answers to her questions.

'Why did you come like this? So late at night?'

'Nature's call' He felt like strangulating her. But strength in his sinews disappeared suddenly. He remained there sitting.

'Why come this way? What is it'?

'Abba! Let me think I dreamt in sleep... Which side is this'?

'West side field.' 'Did I then cross the dam?' 'You appear to be in confusion.' Viyyanna thatha was thinking in himself. Slowly he could remember that he crossed the dam. Gradually he could even remember the person talking to him. The voice was familiar

'Rathi' he said suddenly.

'Did you not recognize it till now?' said Rathi. Thatha got up and stood.

'How is madam?'

Suddenly, house came to memory. The snoring, shivering

and all that. The heart jumped suddenly. 'She is O.K. Tomorrow I shall give her food.'

It felt like life was struggling in him in that darkness. 'Rathi!' he said. Rathi crossed the low bund and went to the other side. Thatha also crossed the bund. She was standing waiting. Thatha embraced her. 'Wait a minute.' Saying so, she was struggling. But somehow, she did not shout loud. Some animal aroused high in thatha. In her, the stubbornness struggled for a while. But the glow of her body, suppressed all these days, established its

might again another time. She surrendered, panting.

Thatha could not recover till the morning star rose. Suddenly he felt like crying. 'Rathi!' he said. 'Thathagaru!' she said.

He set his voice right and sang carelessly, 'Perhaps by

This time my wife might have died.'

'What!' said she, stunned. 'Ayyo, thathagaru! Then let's go.

This time thatha was not afraid of home. He felt like a big weight was removed from him. Because then he was also dead! On the two flanks of the cot, just dead, Rathi and Viyyanna thatha sat till daybreak. Rathi did not look at the dead body at all. She sat looking at Viyyanna thatha in wonder. How brutal he turned in the night! But that night boundless respect and love arose in her for him. She appreciated him that night.

Thatha died that night. But he lived because of Rathi. On the whole, what's to be told is that our thatha's was a strong life. Then imagine that he would go without the knowledge of anybody.

- Translated by Mr.Gopalam Karamchedu
(Rendered from the original story Viyyanna Thatha
Maranam in Telugu)
Published in lokabhiramam.blogspot.com

CHAPTER VI

Headmaster

"Headmaster expired."

Captain Rao read the telegram. He stood still for a while, preoccupied. His wife looked at him with knitted eyebrows. She bent forward to read the telegram in his hand.

"Who is this headmaster?" "Our headmaster."

She shrugged, placed his kerchief and purse on the table, and left the room. Rao stood still, preoccupied. His eyes became misty with old memories.

The sand dunes cut the river Godavari across. From the top of the sand dune, the river looked very weak and pathetic, as if crawling to the end. But once one reached the other side of the dune, she looked livelier and more energetic.

In the river, the headmaster would stand, performing his daily morning "surya namaskaram". Rao was Subba Rao in those days, and his friends, Krishnaiah, Ramanatham, Sambu and Ravi, would swim in the river for about a furlong and go to the other side. There were lots of cucumber creepers on the other side. They hid small packets of chilli powder and salt under the creepers. They would mash the cucumbers with their bare hands and eat them with a blend of chilli powder and salt. From the seeds, which they had spilt while eating routinely, surely led to the sprouting of many more creepers along the shore. By the time they swam back, the headmaster would have finished his surya namaskaram.

"Hello, boys! What are the residents of Kishkindha up to today? Did they bring cucumbers or the melons?" he asked one morning. The boys were taken aback; they never imagined that he knew about their pranks.

"Actually, sir, we were practising swimming," muttered Ramanatham.

"Look here, Satya Harsishchandra! I agree swimming practice is good for you, but if the owner of the grove catches you stealing his cucumbers, he might break your legs, and you won't be able to practice swimming anymore." His humour was very subtle, not stabbing. He would speak softly, emphasising every word leisurely and mildly.

"Hello, Captain Rao? What is wrong with you? You are talking very softly!" It was Captain Reddy on the telephone. Rao smiled to himself. He was imitating the headmaster unconsciously.

In a school play, Rao played the role of Yudhishtira, imitating the headmaster's mannerisms and speech. All the teachers and friends complimented him on the job. The headmaster looked at him with smiling eyes and said, "Subbulu! Finally, you made me Dharmaraja! He was a lousy bastard!" The headmaster was the only person who called him Subbulu.

"Reddy! Can you drop in on your way to the airport? I wish to join you."

"What is the matter?"

"I will tell you later."

Captain Rao returned the telephone to the cradle. He entered the dining room for breakfast. He sat down, sipping orange juice, and still looking vague. His wife, Kamala, threw a suspicious look at him. Both of them have not been on speaking terms for the past month. There was not any fight or argument. In fact, there were no clear-cut accusations either. But Rao knew very well why Kamala was angry and why she shut the bedroom doors on him.

That day, she came to the airport, as usual, to pick him up. She always made it a point to pick him up after his flight duties. She never came after that day. He knew that she wouldn't come anymore. On that day, there was a constant drizzle and wind. He couldn't see her in the pitch-dark night, waiting for him. He did not expect her that day. In fact, she was farthest from his mind. Ms Usha was hanging on to his neck, trying to go down the staircase of the aircraft. It was very uncomfortable on the narrow stairs; he was trying to help her get down, holding her at the waist. Usha felt very giddy as soon as her feet touched the ground (really!). He held tightly to stop her from falling. He helped her into the pickup van and climbed into the van to go with her. It was then that he saw Kamala standing in the rain, under a small umbrella, under one of the wings of the aircraft! It was well past midnight when he reached home, after admitting Usha to the hospital.

Kamala locked herself in the bedroom. A warm welcome indeed his wife had given him after he arrived home, bone tired, exhausted, and traumatised after a brush with death! He tossed and turned on the lounge chair in the living room that entire night. He felt very hurt and indignant at the silent accusation, defending his soul and actions, which were pure as driven snow! Is it fair, he thought, that his wife should suspect him, just because he held a colleague, who was shivering with fright, that too, and whom he treated like his very own sister! (Oh yeah! You held her tender waist with a pressure slightly more than needed. When she put her arms around your neck, her breasts brushing against you, when her heart fluttered like a bird against your chest, when your fingers caressed her spine, and when her hair tickled on your neck, the peculiar pleasure that ran through your nerves was just brotherly!) He bit into the omelette and buttered toast, glancing at his wife. She was observing his absentmindedness intently. She turned her eyes away, unable to bear the love in his eyes anymore. "I need to go to Eluru, disembarking at Vijayawada." She looked at him enquiringly.

"Our headmaster expired. His only son is in the United States. I am like a son to him. His wife will feel happy if I go." He laughed at his own absurd statement. How can a wife be happy with the death of a husband?

Kamala did not laugh. She looked at him as if she had understood what he needed to say.

Rao hesitated for a while and sipped his coffee.

"She doesn't have any kith and kin. Can you accompany me?" Captain Reddy, waiting in the driveway, honked. Rao rose from his chair. Kamala came out of her room, ready to go. He thought her silence meant her reluctance to join him. But she came out, locked the house behind him, and climbed into the van. Reddy gave a questioning look. "The headmaster passed away. We need to go to Eluru." The aircraft was full; no seats for them. He managed to get a place for Kamala in the air hostess' cabin. Reddy was a cool pilot. He steadily lifted the aircraft and onto the cotton-soft clouds.

Rao stood behind him, watching.

The aircraft looked like the centre of the cloud. When it cut across the cloud cover, it sent a funny shiver down the spine. The air hostess, Nayaki, lost her balance but controlled herself.

"I am sorry, I nearly spilt the tea on you," she apologised with a smile.

"I wouldn't mind it if it were only, you spilling on to me, rather than the tea," Reddy joked.

Rao looked at Kamala. His look said, "She is like our sister." He laughed again at his absurd thoughts. He squeezed in to sit beside Kamala.

He slipped into a reverie again. The headmaster was teaching us English. It was an essay by Mahatma Gandhi titled

'All mankind are brethren.' He said, 'Look here, boys. Mahatma seems to be quite a naughty man. He talks only of the males. He deliberately did not mention anything about ladies being our sisters. He must have seen many boys like our Subbulu – that is me. I was quite a naughty boy in my high school days. Kamala's eyes sparkled with a hidden smile. She strongly suspected that Rao said this story just to divert her attention from the air hostess. Though she was partly right, once he started speaking, Rao forgot everything about the air hostess and the conversation. His heart was filled with memories of the headmaster, and his lips parted as he remembered the sweet smile of the headmaster. Kamala gave a sidelong glance at the smile. The second hostess too lost her balance and gave an arrogant smile. Her smile seemed to carry the emptiness one feels in the pit of the stomach when suddenly losing one's footing. She could not guess whether Rao noticed the air hostess or not. Suddenly Rao resumed talking. Air is not like the terra firma. We are used to walking on the firm ground, but flying in the air is always an unpredictable, novel experience, however well trained one is. Air carries the aircraft most of the time. But sometimes, it lets go, like an adult who throws up a child in the air playfully and catches them. At those times, only people who trust the air don't panic. Some pilots do not develop that kind of trust in the air, even after many years of service. On every flight, they consider air as an enemy that needs to be vanquished. Captain Rung-ta was an experienced pilot. He was also a very brave man. But, on that day, he seemed to have lost his mind. That stormy night when Kamala came to receive him at the airport! All of them were nearly killed that night. Captain Rungta was the chief pilot, and Rao was the co-pilot. The left side engine was totally damaged. The wind and storm were tossing the aircraft around as if it was a mere toy. Captain Rungta did the unthinkable. He jumped into an egoistic clash with the storm. The aircraft looked puny and powerless to face nature's fury. The aircraft was spinning like a paper boat. Rao warned Captain Rungta. Rungta yelled back with a gruff "shut up!" Rao was furious. There were about eighty people on the flight who could have died due to Rungta's stupidity. The airport was yet a half mile away. The aircraft steadily started losing height. The small hill ahead of the airport, with a glowing red light on the top of it, was approaching them with alarming speed. "Lift her, lift her!" shouted Rao in panic. Air hostess Usha was screaming in fear and frenzy. In the next two minutes, they would hit the hilltop and crash. Rao lifted his arm and gave a resounding whack on Captain Rungta's neck. Rungta slumped in his seat. Rao pushed him aside and took over the controls. He gave it full throttle and lifted the aircraft. They just crossed the red light by a hair's width. Then he balanced the aircraft steadily in the air. They were almost out of the ruin's way. He made a circular move in the air and slowly landed the aircraft. When, finally, the aircraft came to a halt on the ground, he realised he was swathed in sweat. Usha was clinging on to him and shouting hysterically. He had to take her to the hospital, and only after she was sedated, did she let him go. Rao finished the story.

"The rules and regulations on the ground cannot be taken into consideration while in the air sometimes. I went against the rules when I overpowered Rungta and physically injured him. If I had followed the rules, even when he was prepared to kill all the passengers with his foolishness, I would just stand by and watch. I disregarded the rules because I wanted to save those passengers. Just obeying my instincts is a strong part of my character. Right from my childhood, I caused problems for all those around me with my impulsive nature. On the aircraft, it is a different world altogether. I am the king there. I never make a mistake.

Back on the ground, all I am doing seems to be mistakes. He ignored her on that day and ran to the hospital with Usha, and today, he is trying to justify his actions, thought Kamala. He was not exactly apologising but rather saying that, since he had saved so many lives that night, he had a right to do just what he wanted, she thought foolishly. Rao gave her an understanding smile. He remembered suddenly what the headmaster had said once, "A woman never trusts another woman, and more so, if the woman happens to be close to her husband and, of course, it is the husband whom she trusts the least." Rao completed the rest of the story.

Usha fell asleep on the bed at the hospital. Rao went to the hotel. He sat in his room and wrote a letter to the authorities, explaining his breach of discipline. He mentioned that he hit Captain Rungta and took the controls of the aircraft into his hand. He mentioned that he was willing to accept any punishment given to him. He apologised to Captain Rungta for his behaviour. Captain Rungta stayed in the same hotel, four rooms away. Rao went to his room and knocked on his door. No reply. He glanced at his watch. It was 2:00 a.m. He changed his mind and turned to go when he heard a gruff, "Come in."

The voice sounded heavy with alcohol. Rao entered the room.

"Good evening, my hero!"

The voice was in no way taunting. Rungta glared at him through his blood-red eyes for a while. Rao could not fathom his state of mind. He seemed to be drunk but still in control of his senses. Rao smiled and gave him the letter of apology. Rungta read the letter. He turned away to look at the lamp for a while. Then suddenly he tore up the letter into pieces and threw them into the wastebasket. He again glared at Rao, blankly. Then, he smiled sadly! "Rao, can I get you something to drink? Or are you too tired?" Rao sat down in a chair, ready to serve the drinks. "No, no! You are my guest." Rungta poured the whisky into two glasses.

"Cheers", Rungta emptied his glass. Rao sat silently. He was uncomfortable. Rungta suddenly said, with his eyes shining, "Rao, how could you do it so easily? You saved the aircraft worth nearly eighty lakhs of rupees. More than that, you saved the lives of eighty people, which are priceless. To top it, now you write a letter apologising for your breach of discipline. Oh yes, the blow you gave me on the neck! My neck is all swollen. It will probably hurt more tomorrow! I deserve it, of course. I don't know what had happened to me. I seemed to have gone out of my mind. Somehow, the red lamp was not in my view at all. I thought it was just a matter of time before we all died. My ego sprang up out of nowhere! I got terribly confused. Then you took over. I fell down when you hit me. I got up burning with rage to push you away from the controls. The aircraft that was losing height rapidly suddenly went up and crossed the killer red lamp. How deftly you controlled an aircraft that was running on a single engine!

Your supreme confidence! You turned the aircraft around as if it were a mere bird. Then you landed it gently. I was staring at you. Your eyes, the concentration in them! Then I understood. You hit me not because you hated me or because you were jealous of me. You hit me because you had no other choice at that time. I never knew you could take over the control of a hopeless situation so easily. I always had a very low opinion of you. I assumed you were an irresponsible playboy, joking around with people. Today I know that, behind the happy-go-lucky exterior, lurks a determined, confident professional!" Rao felt terribly embarrassed at the direct admiration and praise. He could not get himself to look at Rungta. He suddenly caught his reflection in the mirror on the dressing table. It looked strange! It suddenly turned into the headmaster's face! He was amazed to find the same eyes, looking innocent with all the wisdom behind them, and the same smile. Suddenly, he realised that the headmaster had become a part of himself. He knew he could never be the same person as the headmaster was. The headmaster would never get into trouble, like he did, always. He would pull people out of troubles! When he himself got into many troubles, it was the headmaster who pulled him out. On that night too, it was the headmaster who took control, thought Rao." Rao, I am quitting. I can no longer be a pilot." "Nonsense," protested Rao.

"Rao, I had been a pilot of fighter planes during many wars. I escaped many mortal dangers. I know very well how calm and courageous a pilot must be, how he needs to keep his cool in the face of dangers. I lost those qualities. If I feel wobbly when the aircraft is out of control, I can no longer be a pilot. Tomorrow I will meet the chairman and request him to transfer me into the administrative section. If he refuses, I shall resign. "Rao knew that Rungta spoke the truth. He sighed. Rungta got up on his bed. "I am terribly sleepy, Rao. You can stay if you like and finish the drink. If you need it, there is one more bottle in the fridge. I never expected to see you tonight. I am so happy!" Rungta fell asleep even before Rao finished saying "good night".

Kamala looked at him. His arm circled her waist. She gave a cautious look around. Both the air hostesses seemed to be missing. The aircraft started descending. "No seat belt here", Rao gripped her waist firmly. "Those poor girls are missing their chances because of me", she said, tauntingly. But there was no malice in her voice. She choked when the wheels touched the ground. She felt secure and happy with his arms holding her. When they were in the taxi en route to Eluru, Rao opened his diary and showed it to her. Under the plastic wrapper, there was a photograph, which she had never seen before. "Who is this?"

"Our headmaster."

She looked at the picture for a long time. The dead body was placed in the main hall. The headmaster's wife sat at his feet. Janardana Rao and his daughter Nagamani sat a few feet away. "Hello, Subba Rao," Janardana Rao recognised him. Nagamani looked at him and turned away. The headmaster's wife looked at him vacantly.

"Subba Rao, Surya Rao (headmaster's son) will not be here for three days, at least. We need to cremate the body before it starts decaying. What do you think we should do?" asked Janardana Rao. Rao went to the headmaster's wife.

"Madam, can I perform the last rites? I am like your own son," his voice choked. She gave him a blank look. Finally, she said, "Alright, child!" Janardana Rao got busy with the arrangements. Rao refused to look at the headmaster's lifeless face. He firmly retained, in his mind, only the living, lively face of his teacher. As he walked along the streets, performing the last rites, he felt the streets calling to him, silently. Rao remembered: The memories of the canal, the shore, the boats, and the early morning when I stole bananas and jaggery from the boats swarmed my mind. Mother sent me to Kovvoor to study in the high school. The headmaster of the high school and my father were childhood friends. Mother was very much worried about my mischievous deeds. I stayed in a small room next to the headmaster's house with three other friends. I was at an age when rebellion came naturally to me. I could not fathom the headmaster for the first few days. With grey hair, a moustache, and gold-framed glasses, he indeed looked academic. He would sit on the verandah till late at night, in his armchair, reading a book. One day, I took the other boys to a late-night show at the circus tent. The other boys were good as long as they were on their own; they would never go for a late-night circus show. They would not tell tales about me to the headmaster either. The next day, when we were swimming in Godavari, the headmaster asked, "Boys, how was the circus last night?"

By the time I gathered my wits to bluff my way out, the headmaster had already left. I realised that I would never be able to lie to him. The cremation fire was glowing. Janardana Rao and he sat on the shore of the canal. "I have never seen anyone think so clearly and be so good at heart. I shifted to Eluru for Nagamani's education.

He too retired and settled here. His son went abroad. He would always ask me, 'Dear sir! Please find a small house for my old woman and me. I can't afford high rents.' I got him to stay in this house. We would meet every day. Both of them liked Nagamani very much." "Did Nagamani get married, sir?" Rao asked hesitantly. Janardana Rao smiled. "Of course! She is of the same age as you are. It was he who saved you and her after the big furore. I was hell-bent upon ruining your future in those days. He diffused the whole situation. Of course, it was good for my daughter too ..." Janardana Rao was a member of the Brahmo Samaj. Their ancestors were from the courtesans' caste. He was a lawyer by profession and got all his sisters married. Nagamani was his eldest daughter. She was my classmate. She was very proud of her father and always spoke of "her dad". He always quoted from scriptures. Most of the high-caste Hindus ridiculed him. Our Telugu teacher always joked about him. Ramanatham and Sambu always walked behind the girls after school and teased them with comments.

"Who could be the father of the lawyer?"

"It is a bit difficult to tell. You would have to choose from many people!"

"Unfortunately, he wants to become a respectable man." "No point in washing a rat's skin; it is forever black," they would sing.

Nagamani would be enraged and treat all of us like filth. One day a Telugu teacher said in the staff room,

"All the great people in the Mahabharata are of dubious parentage! Like some respectable people in our town."

The headmaster just then entered the room and said mildly, "Now, sir, do you think one knows surely who one's father is? We have to go just by what our mothers say, don't we? In any case, we are in no way affected by who our father is but by who we are, don't you think?" One day in the evening, Janardana Rao was giving us a talk in the school. The headmaster invited him. We all got angry with both of them. When he stood up to give his talk, we made a racket. He seemed to be slightly irritated, but our headmaster looked calm. Janardana Rao, unable to finish his talk, concluded as early as he could. The headmaster got up to say something. We were all waiting nervously. He said without any emotion, "I wish to thank Mr Janardana Rao on behalf of all of us. The thanks are not for his talk. It is for his patience towards us. I also apologise to him, for I could not teach basic courtesy to my students."

All the teachers sitting in the front looked uncomfortable. All of us understood how pained the headmaster was with the emphasis he placed on each word. With our childhood irrationality, we held Janardana Rao responsible for all the agony of the evening. To add to it, Nagamani abused us with strong words. I was even more enraged. When I found her alone, I started taunting her about her caste. She would turn red in the face but never complained to any of the teachers. Perhaps, she guessed correctly that none of the teachers would support her. One fine day, she gave a sarcastic smile and quoted the proverb, Elephants always ignore the barking dogs. That day, the history class was the last class. The history teacher was a pious, timid old man. We loved to embarrass him with silly questions. We found his discomfort hilarious. That day, I made Sambu ask him how many concubines Krishnadeva Rayalu could have had. Our history teacher turned red in the face since he held Krishnadeva Rayalu in high respect. Fortunately, the bell rang and put him out of his misery. He rushed to leave the class. After going out, he must have remembered that the teacher who taught in the last hour should wait till all the girls in the class left. I did not notice him standing outside the entrance. All the boys were in a stampede near the entrance. The girls waited for all the boys to leave. At the end of the girls was Nagamani, standing. She gave her usual sarcastic smile to me. I lost my temper. All the girls were moving out. In the end, Nagamani was behind her. Suddenly, on an impulse, I grabbed her plaited hair in my hand and pulled her towards me. She screamed in fright and fell over me. I held her waist and hugged her. I do not know why I did. All the girls were screaming hysterically. The teacher came inside the class shouting, "You naughty boy! What are you up to? "I fled the scene. I ran without aim or direction along the river. I climbed the railway bridge and ran towards Rajahmundry. Some train entered the railway bridge and was moving towards me. I ran till I reached the next station. My lungs were bursting with exertion. I slumped on the platform. I reached home by ten o'clock at night. I stood near the wall in the darkness. I heard Janardana Rao speaking to the headmaster. "We have to teach such rowdies a stiff lesson. I will see to it that he is kicked out of the school forever. "Sure, sir! I will file a complaint with the higher office. I shall write a strong complaint so that he cannot join any other school. Let the history teacher come with the report first," said the headmaster. I felt weak in my legs and slumped down. Janardana Rao left after a while. The headmaster saw him off at the gate, turned back to go in, and noticed me. I stood up facing him.

He slapped me on the face. I fell down and could not get up again. He came down to look into my face. He said, "Go inside and sleep." He paused again before going in and asked, "Have you eaten any food?" I did not answer. He took me inside. He called his wife and said, "I think this idiot has not had any food. Give him something to eat." I wondered if she knew what I had done. I said I did not want any food.

The headmaster said, "Shut up and eat."

I ate my food and looked at him. He looked like God, who could forgive all our sins. I finished the food and came out. He was reading a book on his chair. I wanted to tell him something but could gather neither my wits nor courage. He simply said, "Go to bed now."

I went inside my room. Both my roommates, too, did not talk to me. I promptly went to bed. I could not sleep, and my brain was teeming with absurd thoughts. I have to apologise to Nagamani. Of course, I will be rusticated from the school. Then I will humiliate her again in the main street. Why did I do it? What will happen to me now? What will Mother say? I will commit suicide. The whole night, dreams haunted me. The next morning, I did not go to the Godavari for my usual swim. I did not step out of my room. My roommates still avoided me, as if I were a harmful animal. I heard the history teacher talking outside to the headmaster. "Idiots, these boys are! We have to punish him, sir. How dare he be in the class with so many students! I tell you, sir, he should be...."

I peeped through the crack in the door to see what was going on. The history teacher wrote a three-page report, which the headmaster was reading. He read the first page and merely turned the rest of the two pages. "That is fine, sir. I will report the incident to the higher authorities," he said in the end. A week went by. Every evening Janardana Rao would come and ask about the status of the complaint. "Come on, sir. How can we discipline the schoolchildren if we don't punish the rascals? Why there is no reply for your complaint?"

"Red tape, sir! Do you think any office works efficiently in our country? Most of the time they simply throw our letters in the wastepaper basket," the headmaster would say. "Please send them a reminder."

"Sure. I will do it right away. I will mark a copy to the D.E.O. too!"

Every morning, the history teacher would come to make similar enquiries. Again, the same dialogue would go on. I kept imagining what would happen next. The headmaster would write a reminder. It would travel by the evening mail to Eluru. The D.E.O. would read the letter. He would call Mother and tell her the matter. How upset she would be! If only the letter would not reach Eluru! If the train meets with an accident near Nidadavolu! If only all the letters would catch fire! Or, if the letter would be read by a clerk in the D.E.O.'s office, who was in a similar predicament in his younger days! He would sympathise with me and throw the report in the rubbish. I heard that Nagamani had not been coming to school for the past four days. I felt guilty. After ten days, the history teacher came in the early morning, in a bad mood. "What is this I hear, sir? It seems you never sent that report to the higher authorities." The headmaster fell silent for a minute.

"Hmmm! Actually, I am having second thoughts about sending the letter."

"What? How can you spare such undisciplined brats? How could you forgive him?"

"Come on, sir! Is he an enemy soldier to hate him so much? He is still a child!"

"What are you saying, sir? How will we train the children if we let him go?"

"Dear Sir, all those sages who performed strict penances and thought nothing beyond God's feet too ran agog with desire when they saw an apsara. Why talk of a young, inexperienced boy! I do not know about you, sir, but honestly, if a good-looking girl were passing by, I too would feel extremely tempted to give a second look!

The fear of the society, my family, and my own concepts of good and bad all together pull me back. Or else, I too would have hugged a girl of my age. I do not, because I know that in that event, more than the girl, I will be in soup. He is a young boy; he did not have such discerning capacity. He made a small mistake. Who knows how much he is repenting now? If we leave him now, he will never do such a thing in all his life. If we ruin his life by expelling him from the school, he may never get a chance to start afresh. His repentance is his own punishment, I think."

Suddenly they both were in my room. I was slumped on the floor. I could not lift up my head with the weight of guilt. Slowly both of them left. That day evening the lawyer came as usual. After some routine discussions, he got up to go. "Sir, I need to tell you something. I took my own decision in a small matter. I did not send the report to the higher authorities," said the headmaster. "But why?" said the lawyer. I heard a roar in my ears;

The anxiety and the pressure were too much to bear. He was saying, "If you complain about me, I will have to resign from my job. In principle, I should have filed that report and punished that boy. But somehow, I was not convinced about the wisdom of the action. I am a teacher. When one of my students strays, my duty is to show him the right path, not ruin his life. If I had sent a report about his misbehaviour, he would have been expelled from the school, which of course he deserves. But he will be totally out of control then. He might think he can do anything and get away with it. He might even humiliate your daughter even more! You can get him arrested, but then unnecessary rumours will start floating about your daughter too, which I think is undesirable. But if you insist, I shall send the report." "That's fine, but why did you not tell me for such a long time?"

"You were too enraged to think calmly. "After that, I lost track of their conversation.

I ran out of the house. I took a shortcut to reach the lawyer's house before him. I was breathless when I reached their house. I knocked on their door.

His wife opened the door and asked, "Yes, who is it?"

"It's me, Subba Rao. She gasped. She became stiff as if I were some murderer or a drunkard.

Nagamani came out.

"You!" she said." I am very sorry, Nagamani. I did something very wrong. I am not asking you to forgive me. I do not know why I behaved so badly."

I did not notice the lawyer standing behind me. I turned back to go home and saw him. "Sir, I heard all that you and the headmaster were talking. I am sorry for what I have done. Even if you get me expelled, I will not bother Nagamani anymore. Do what you think is the best, sir".

I did not return home that night. I sat in the schoolyard. I slept there. From the next day, I attended school as usual. Everybody seemed to have forgotten about the incident. I cleared my school leaving exams in flying colours that year. I thought that was the best way to thank the headmaster. I wanted him to have the satisfaction of pulling a man from the brink of ruin. After that, whenever I faced a problem, I would think about what the headmaster would have expected me to do. He became my alter ego. When I make stupid mistakes, my alter ego lovingly forgives me and corrects me gently.

He sat on the cot and told the entire story to Kamala. Nagamani was sleeping inside with her mother. In the mild light of the dawn, all the birds were waking up the entire world. He looked at Kamala sleeping peacefully, her head perched on his thigh. A smile played on her lips, a smile that knows all his faults, just like the headmaster's smile.

Translated by Ms.Sharada, Australia,
(Rendered from the original story Head Mastaru in Telugu)
Published in www.thulika.net

CHAPTER VII

Honest Hustler

There are about eight magistrate courts in its precincts. I am supposed to appear as a witness in Court 6. The policeman TS-163, who brought me here, is not addressed by name but by his staff ID number. He pointed at my court with his hand and left, perhaps for tea. There is not an inch of space in the court; it is crowded with people connected to other petty cases. There is some space on the two benches, but those benches are reserved for lawyers. Even if there were space, we are not allowed to sit. I came out of the courtroom, as there was no other choice.

The scorching heat of May's sun is severe on the face. Inside, the magistrate was listening attentively as a middle-aged woman described in Tamil, in a somewhat raspy and assuaged voice, how a particular person lured her, undressed her, and did the rest.

Meanwhile, a shopkeeper outside was about to beat up a lawyer but was prevented by four onlookers. He furiously showered invectives towards the lawyer's mother, wife, and other female relatives. The said lawyer allegedly collected the fee from him, later colluded with the police, and got him fined one hundred and fifty rupees. I couldn't grasp the crime entirely. I don't have the desire or the patience to delve into it. I was very thirsty. Standing in the slim shade in front of a street-side kiosk, I sipped soda for fifteen long minutes until the kiosk owner showed irritation.

There are many trees providing shade on the premises, but there is no scope to stand under those trees, as thousands of ants have built anthills and established colonial dominance. If any other species trespasses, they will attack in self-defence.

My case is a three-year-old one. One night, by opening the latch of the bedroom with his tact, a thief stole two tape recorders and one hundred and fifty rupees from a drawer. When I got up in the morning, I was furious and anxious, called the police, and got them home. I wrote down the complaint with the details of the lost items and was so satisfied as if the lost items were recovered. After that, I gradually forgot about it. A year ago, the police brought the thief along with two tape recorders to our house. The product numbers on them matched the numbers in my report. I was glad to find my tape recorders! The efficiency of the police did surprise me. But I was given to understand by the police that court authorisation has to be obtained after the trial is concluded! The police said they would inform me the date of posting of the case and asked me present at the court.

What I came to know subsequently is that the thief, Veeraswamy, elsewhere in the town, a year and a half ago, had entered a house and, while attempting to steal a gold chain from an old woman's neck, killed her. While investigating the murder, the police retrieved, along with the old woman's gold chain, various other things like tape recorders, watches, mixers, and briefcases stolen from other houses. Apart from the crime of murder, there are eight other minor cases against him. He was sentenced to life for murder. The remaining eight cases are yet to be tried and sentenced.

One evening when I returned home exhausted, I saw the court's summons: I must appear in the 6th Magistrate's Court the next day. Hoping to get the tape recorders back, my family members coaxed me to go to the court. I went at ten and waited till three in the evening for the arrival of Veeraswamy, with a police escort! He was to be brought here from a jail in another town. Meanwhile, some hurdle came in the way of bringing Veeraswamy to the court, and the government pleader asked the magistrate to adjourn the case. The magistrate adjourned the case and posted it for hearing after a month without taking into consideration my hardships, if any. On the second date of convening the case, the police produced Veeraswamy. Even if he confesses to the crime or if the court sentences him, in all the remaining eight cases, this period of punishment will not be over and above the period of life imprisonment but be limited to that. Hence, the magistrate advised him to confess in all the other cases to avoid prolonged trials. Veeraswamy smiled and said that he should not be denied the right to defend each case! This time Veeraswamy sought a postponement. The magistrate agreed, and again without seeking my stance or opinion, the case was posted for hearing again after a month or so.

After a firm resolve not to go further to the hearings, I have witnessed four more adjournments! My case continued to get postponed. Surely this is the final hearing, and the police made me come to the court. The government pleader taught me what to testify in front of the magistrate. In that briefing, he explained to me that I must confirm and authenticate in front of the magistrate about 'one' tape recorder being stolen, its company name, and number. I asked him, "What about the second tape recorder?" The pleader and the police acted as if they had not heard about it at all! Standing in the sun waiting for Veeraswamy's arrival made both my body and mind tired and fatigued. Veeraswamy was brought with royal decorum and made to sit in a cool shed. Veeraswamy was presented in the court around two-thirty in the afternoon after he was served his lunch. After half an hour or so, they called me in. I was overwhelmed with hunger, thirst, and anger, and I could not hear their call. A stranger, who was standing next to me, smoking leisurely a beedi, patted me on the shoulder and said, "Go in. They are calling you!" I didn't understand how he knew my name.

I felt giddy as soon as I stepped into the courtroom. I felt like lying down and sleeping in the witness box itself. The bench clerk made me pronounce the all-too-familiar oaths. It was then the government lawyer made me briefly spell out the details of the theft in my house through his questioning. In the questioning that followed later, the magistrate asked, "Can you recognise Veeraswamy, who is standing in front of you, who stole one (with emphasis on one!) tape recorder from your bedroom? Is he the same person whom the police brought to your house the other day?"

The fact that the lawyer emphasised in an earlier briefing the theft of only one tape recorder, not two, made me cringe. My suppressed irritation, anger, and helplessness were about to blurt out. "I don't know," I replied, controlling my annoyance. The magistrate repeated the question.

"Can I remember the face that I saw for maybe ten minutes, two years ago?" I questioned the magistrate.

I was warned that I should only reply to the questions asked by the magistrate and not ask a counter question.

I swore before God that I would tell the truth and asserted that I cannot tell a lie. I am not certain whether Veeraswamy was the person brought that day to my house.

Veeraswamy flashed a proud smile at the court officials.

The government lawyer and the police went into a huddle for a while. Then a tape recorder was placed in front of me.

The lawyer asked if it was mine. I said, "Yes, it is mine."

"Where is the proof?" the lawyer queried.

"The company name and product number will be there on it. Please check," I replied. The lawyer said that the name of the company is there, but not the number. He said it has been erased. After that, the lawyer accused me of colluding with Veeraswamy and telling lies to protect him. I became angry.

"What are these courts meant for? What justice could one get here?" I said in desperation. "If the person who lost the money and goods is made a criminal, made to stand in the sun, and subjected to torture. One of my two tape recorders that I lost was usurped by the police, and the other one produced in the court is certified that it is not mine. What justice could I aspire for?"

In that rage, I derided all the courts, the police establishment, and the lawyer community. The rage turned into despondency when the magistrate sentenced me to remain in the court till it rises for the day for contempt of court.

"Hmmm! As a criminal I can at least be within the court instead of getting baked in the sun outside!" I said bitterly. But no one seemed to be stirred by my utterances and demeanour.

I went and sat hesitantly next to Veeraswamy on the bench. How true? All criminals are equal in the eyes of the court! As I sat next to Veeraswamy, he smiled and said in English, "You are a fool!" It sounded so true. I pitied myself for my plight.

"Look at that court hustler. Learn from him!" said Veeraswamy, pointing to the person standing on the other side.

I could recognise him. He was the same person who patted my shoulder and directed me into the court in the afternoon. I had seen him each time in the court during my last four or five visits. I thought he was either a clerk under a lawyer or a person belonging to the police establishment.

The police produced him as a prosecution witness after me. His testimony was very convincing. He testified under oath that Veeraswamy himself was the thief who was brought to his house. He said in a nonchalant tone that the tape recorder in the hands of the lawyer belonged to him and that it was what was stolen from his house by Veeraswamy. The court was convinced that the tape recorder belonged to him and that Veeraswamy had stolen it from his house. No matter how many counter questions Veeraswamy posed, he did not budge and replied convincingly.

Until the court concluded for the day, Veeraswamy explained to me about this court hustler's enviable tact and presence of mind. He extends his 'professional witness' services not just to the police but also to petty criminals for a fee. His testimony, irrespective of its veracity, was taken seriously by the courts because of his consistent and convincing demeanour. I listened to Veeraswamy with bewilderment.

When the court finally adjourned, I was allowed to leave. I walked out into the open, feeling both relieved and bitter. The thought of getting back my stolen tape recorders seemed remote now. As I stepped outside, the sun was setting, casting long shadows over the premises. I pondered over the day's events and my encounter with the magistrate.

I didn't feel like going home. I felt as if I had done something wrong and didn't want to show my face at home. My self-esteem was deeply hurt.

Meanwhile, the magistrate came out of the court and was boarding an autorickshaw. I went closer to him and greeted him with a namaskaram. He humbly bowed and asked, "Who are you?"

"I was sentenced for contempt of court three hours ago by your majesty," I said impudently, giving vent to my suppressed emotions.

"Have you forgotten me so soon"?" I asked the magistrate in a sardonic tone.

"When I testified in your courtroom that I didn't remember the face of the thief, that I saw briefly two years ago, I was accused of intentional lying!"

He glared at me as if I were a crazy person and boarded the autorickshaw and left.

Deeply sighing, I left for home.

Meanwhile, someone called me loudly by my name. I stopped and looked back. The person who called me was none other than the court hustler! He came in a hurry and handed over the tape recorder to me. I did not foresee such a happening. He prodded me to get an autorickshaw and leave.

Meanwhile, a constable came running towards us. He asked in Tamil to hand over the tape recorder. The court hustler replied that it belonged to him, and even if the top number was erased, the original number was still there on the battery case. He brazenly told him to check it if he wished to! I was filled with awe at his acuity! I wasn't aware of this and had never so minutely explored it! The constable stood there stunned by the hustler's volte-face. Meanwhile, the autorickshaw arrived. The court hustler also boarded the auto along with me! I didn't anticipate this.

I was blamed for colluding with Veeraswamy inside the court, and now I could be accused of running away with the court hustler! That thought baffled my mind.

The autorickshaw was going steadily through the maze of traffic. I tried to pass the tape recorder back to him.

"You are so naive," he quipped. "If this is in our house, the police will come and seize it and make a false case that I stole your tape recorder and call you to testify!" His subtle knowledge of likely police machinations overwhelmed me. He refused to take the tape recorder back. "Let your tape recorder be with you," he said unwaveringly.

"Will the police let you go if you give me this tape recorder?" I asked. "They don't chase or harass me! Even if they do, I am not afraid, as they will not be able to find the tape recorder in my house once I hand it over to you. Why do I fear?" he said confidently.

"Then will the police call you in the future to testify? Will you not lose your livelihood?" I asked.

"They need me, not the other way around," he said assuredly.

"Moreover, I am not too solicitous or interested in police cases. I get paid a meagre ten or twenty rupees, whereas for a private case, I would get a hundred to two hundred rupees depending on the case," he said, asserting his confidence in his professional ability. I tried to offer a hundred-rupee currency bill to him. He said with folded hands, gesturing namaskaram, "I can't accept a payoff for returning your own belonging! It would suffice if you let me travel up to Mount Road."

"Standing in a witness box and speaking falsehood is for my livelihood. Will God pardon me, Sir, if I am not just and honest, at least outside the court arena?" the court hustler reasoned.

Regardless of the court hustler's avocation in the court, I was very pleased to learn about his moral convictions. I developed envy as well as reverence for him. He took leave of me at Mount Road.

I held closely the recovered 'one' tape recorder! The autorickshaw sped towards my home.

- Translated by Dr. Palagummi Sasidhar
(Nephew of Shri Palagummi Padmaraju)
(Rendered from the original story Courttupakshi
written by Palagummi Padmaraju in Telugu)

CHAPTER VIII

Tomorrow, My Birthday

"Tomorrow is my birthday; I will be sixty tomorrow."

Leaning far back into the cushions of his luxurious car, 'Paramita' looked at the treetops that were flying backwards, the sky slit into fragments by those treetops and the bits of white cloud deep inside the sky that moved motionlessly along with his car. It was not exactly them he was looking at. He was trying to probe into them to locate some formless forms, whose contours had almost disappeared. There was a time when he shied away from the name 'Paramita', a name by which his disciples referred to him both on the platform and in the press, in those days when he started interpreting the mind and the teachings of the Great Buddha, having drunk deep at the fountain of that wisdom. He thought that pen names were a little pompous and in bad taste. But the name was associated with his achievements and his fame during a whole decade, and when he published his essays in book form, he put down the name of the author as 'Paramita'. His disciples were pleasantly surprised and even a little intrigued. Some of them, motivated by mischievous curiosity, asked him why he accepted that name. He replied, with a benevolent smile, that however great a man was, he had to bow down before the weight of public opinion. From among the bits of white cloud, there emerged a form, rare and fascinating, and stood before his mind's eye. It was the form of his cousin Ramadevi when she was young and full of vitality. The golden yellow complexion of the ripe betel leaf, the hair parted above her left eyebrow where the tender hair curled into a spiral like a small whirlpool, the plaited hair with the dark blue sheen reaching almost to her knees and lifted by the ample curve beneath the small of her back, and the large innocent-looking eyes with the dark eyebrows and the lovely squint, all were there as clearly as if she were there in flesh and blood. He felt he could touch her if he stretched his hand. She had a knack of smiling with the squint of her eyes, and you felt as if you were enveloped in a cool, bracing summer shower. But it was difficult to know for whom the shower was meant on account of the squint. He had a suspicion that even at that early age, she realised the possibilities of that squint and that she deliberately made use of it purely for fun. Ramadevi was now in her early fifties. She had five or six children. Her hair turned grey. Even the eyebrows were spotted with grey. Now she parted her hair in the middle. But the permanent curl above the left eyebrow was still there, as though it symbolised some unchanging trait in her character. The squint also was there, lovely but confusing as of old. His disciples were making preparations to celebrate his sixtieth birthday on a grand scale. He once again had to bow down before the weight of public opinion and accept the invitation. He would be seated on a pedestal, like the duplicate image of God used on ceremonial occasions, and there would be long speeches in his praise, full of meaningless commonplaces. He closed his eyes in acute discomfort at the thought. A lorry passed in the opposite direction, raising a huge cloud of dust and sound, and he was again conscious of his surroundings. A few yards ahead, the road to Nidadavole (town in East

Godavari district) branched off to the right from the main road. Turn to the right, Chenchiah said.

Chenchiah always did what he was told to do and never asked for any explanations. That was why he stuck to Chenchiah for over twenty years. Servants were replaced; cooks were replaced. Even friendships did not endure long. The unmitigated monotony of constancy tired him. He could not stand even his own house, not to mention his own village, for any length of time. Have you never loved anyone? Why were you not married?

A disciple had asked him once. I would have gone mad looking at the same face day in and day out for so many years, he had replied. His disciples felt free to put him any question they liked; he put them so much at their ease, and there was nothing formal in his relationship with them. Even so, he never thought of replacing Chenchiah. Whatever you told him, Chenchiah's face never showed any reaction. He merely did what he was told to do. Chenchiah knew many of his secrets. Many foolish things had happened in this back seat of the car. There were occasions when he made an utter fool of himself over others, and others made themselves fools over him. But Chenchiah never gave an indication, even by a look, that he knew those things happened. But Chenchiah was neither dull-witted nor stupid. His was the immobility of a sharp and intelligent mind. There was something in Chenchiah that was akin to the essence of Buddhism – the 'Paramita', a state of being which knows all but transcends knowledge. He had, for Chenchiah, an affection not unmixed with gratitude. Chenchiah was his companion during all the ups and downs of his high-strung life, but Chenchiah remained aloof, untouched by them, like the proverbial drop of water on the lotus leaf. Chenchiah stopped the car in front of Ramadevi's house. He knew what he should do without being told. "Uncle has come!" shouted Rangappa, Ramadevi's fourth son. Rangappa resembled his mother closely. They sent us an invitation for your birthday celebrations, said Ramadevi. I am going to Rajahmundry in that connection. I dropped in just to see you on the way, he said. What do you mean? Are you indicating that you do not want me to come? asked Ramadevi. He was unable to decide whether she said it in fun or in seriousness.

"You are devoid of form, but the twinkle in the corners of your eyes is where all forms are born."

It was from a poem he had written about her in those mad days of youth. The lines came to him in a sudden flash. He looked at her. Tomorrow he will be completing sixty years. Tomorrow is a festive day. All his disciples would be awaiting his arrival with anxiety and enthusiasm. They would have prepared the dais with taste. Tomorrow is not the same as every other day. Tomorrow is different. Tomorrow is unique.

Once he was twenty-five. Then he had a whole future spread out in front of him. Many people offered their daughters to him in marriage with spectacular dowries. He contemptuously laughed at those offers. Marriage was not for the likes of him. Marriage was for the ordinary male – for the likes of Manikyam.

Manikyam was the same age as he. He had only two passions in his life then: food and sleep.

Rama was a destitute child. Her mother had passed away. Her father squandered all his property on drink. His father gave her shelter and succour. She grew up under the same roof as he for ten years.

A huge sprawling affair was that house, built in four quarters, the roof sloping down to the centre of each quarter into an iron pipe which served as a drain for rainwater. The southern yard was bounded on all sides by high walls. There was an overgrown jasmine creeper in the yard. A huge tamarind tree brushed its trunk against the northern wall, slowly eating into the wall, the branches unsettling the tiles of the roof when there was a breeze. Rama and he used to climb onto the roof and eat the tender tamarind fruit. They used to hide small packets of salt under the tiles of the roof. Rama used to dip the tamarinds into salt and crunch them happily under her teeth. He also used to munch tamarinds. But his teeth ached on account of the loss of enamel; the tamarinds were so sour, and he could not eat his food afterwards. But Rama could eat her food with relish after the tamarinds.

Uncle, that was Rama's father used to visit his home whenever he needed money for his drink. My father used to spurn him in utter disgust, but in the end, he always used to give him some money. Uncle never made his appearance again till the money was spent. On occasions, when Uncle came home drunk, Rama put him to sleep with touching affection. She patiently listened to all his drunken babble, and when he sank into his intoxicated slumber, she covered him with a blanket, put off the light, came out and talked with us as if nothing had happened. On the day of her marriage, Uncle did not turn up to give the bride away.

Later, it became known that he was lying drunk in the temple yard. My parents had to oversee the wedding formalities of Rama.

The sacred disc of Vishnu on the top of the temple was askew, and the mud walls of the compound were almost washed down. The carved stones slipped from their places here and there. There was a row of yellow 'Ganneru' trees around the temple. Nambi Achary, the priest, bathed in the temple tank every day and brought sacred water in a huge polished brass vessel over which he painted the 'namam', which was the symbol of Lord Vishnu. He ('Paramita') and Rama spent many evenings in the temple yard. They discussed many questions and often disagreed. Was Subbanna's wife good or bad? Why did Gopalam, the karanam, always cough? Did Venkamma really elope with Veeraswamy?

Tomorrow, I will be completing sixty years. I have not lived in vain. I have given so much to the world. I have cut my heart into bits and presented them to the world in the form of my writings; I have suffered that the world might be happy. I have borne the burden of the world's sorrows and its unfulfilled desires so that the world might live a fuller life. I know the world, but the world does not know me. It only knows my name, and it raises memorials to that name. It does not know there is 'me', apart from the name. That other 'I' is crushed and sapped dry under the weight of the world's miseries. It is out of untold suffering that all art emerges, but it gives the world only happiness.

Rama and her husband were in the back seat of the car happily discussing commonplaces, hurling childish jokes at each other. Yes, people who live by moneylending never grow up with their age. Rama's temperament was also that of a moneylender. When he read his poems to her, she always laughed. She liked good food, good clothing, and glittering jewels. The land of the Moon and the garden of Indra simply did not exist for her. In a way, she was happily married. Her husband also had similar tastes and temperament. Why don't you marry Rama?' his father had asked him. He laughed away the suggestion and gave a lengthy dissertation on marriage as a social institution. Having heard him through, his father had asked again, that is all right, but are you willing to marry Rama?

He could not find a satisfactory answer to that question till Rama was married to her present husband. Strange that Rama, who knew about this unanswered question, never even casually referred to it when they were alone. Had she so much as set the ball rolling, he would have laid bare his heart to her. But she merely sat on the roof beside him, crunching tamarinds and salt under her teeth. On the day of the marriage, he suffered agonies and, till the last moment, was hoping that some miracle would stop it. That night he had many dreams, all about the marriage being stopped. Supposing he had married Rama. What then? His mind shook with spontaneous laughter. He would have sat at the moneylender's table, making elaborate calculations, would have become the father of five or six children, and would have been beside her in the back seat of the car playing childish pranks. Then, who would be there to present to the world the 'Prajna Paramita'? Who would be there to become the teacher of this huge band of disciples? Art demands the unqualified surrender of its devotee. It accepts the sacrifice of his all or nothing. The artist annihilates himself and gives the world eternal happiness. A thousand Ramas cannot equal a poem. What if all art is annihilated? If the world is peopled by Ramas, where is the need for art? Is art greater, or life? Life, of course – what doubt is there! All art strives to make that one point. That is the message of art. Then how foolish it is to sacrifice life for the sake of art! Life, experience of living – that is the essence of human existence. After all, art is dead; life must be alive. Yes. Tomorrow is my birthday. The car stopped in front of the Gouthami Library. Rama and her husband got down from the back seat. He was asleep in the front seat beside the driver, Chenchiah. Involuntary tears were running down his cheeks. Rama woke him up. He got up and wiped his eyes and face.

Tomorrow is my birthday; tomorrow I will be sixty.

Translated by Shri Palagummi Padmaraju
(Rendered from the original story Phalasruthi in Telugu)
Published in Triveni magazine – 1957

CHAPTER IX

Granny Is Dead

The pyre was ready. The purohit asked Pani for the umpteenth time what Granny's name was, and Pani mechanically repeated it. He had a little difficulty in pronouncing 'Lakshmikanthamma'; it sounded different each time he uttered it. He had started to imbibe the previous day what they call patta and never stopped until we forced the pot of fire into his hands and made him walk in front of the body. 'Lash...mi...mma,' he said once again to forestall the purohit's question. How hare-brained these purohits were! They could not remember a name for two seconds! Lakshmikanthamma-Suramma-Perammanam' chanted the purohit. Suramma was Granny's mother-in-law, and Peramma was Suramma's mother-in-law; they were the daughters-in-law of the house in reverse order. Funny, trying to offer rice and water to disembodied spirits! I had a fleeting vision of Granny's spirit hovering about the Palmyra tree in the crematorium, looking on at the ritual with her cool, enigmatic smile, a smile utterly devoid of mockery or even criticism. It always exuded benevolence, goodness and humanity. That smile had a personality. It filled one with peace and happiness. We moved into the house beside the level crossing on a working day, and so I could not attend to the shifting of our belongings. My wife managed it with the help of our servants and the lorry hands. When I returned to my new home after a busy day at the office, I felt peeved at the volume of junk, my wife had collected during the six months of our stay in Bombay. When I left Bombay to take up my assignment in the new unit that our company had started in Madras. I very cleverly managed to dispose of all the rubbish she had gathered there. I sent her to Madras, a few days ahead of me, with our items of clothing, a radiogram and a deal wood box of cooking paraphernalia. The rest of our belongings I sold or gave away, and I landed in Madras with only my suitcase and a sense of fulfilment.

My wife was, of course, furious that I could have brought myself to part with the stone mortar (her mother's gift), the broom with the long handle (her proud purchase in Chembur) and a hundred other items, each of which had as long a history as the Asoka Pillar. So, I stepped into the hall and saw a huge assortment of stone and wooden pestles, a dozen varieties of sieves, rolling pins, broken glass jars filled with such odd items as beads, toothpicks and used blades, moth-eaten photographs, rusted steel trunks, baskets, deal wood boxes and what not. I felt sick with despair. 'In another hour, you will not find anything here,' my wife sought to reassure me.

'Why don't you vacate it as yet?' she said, and went about her business of arranging things. It is impossible to maintain a pose of irritation without some cooperation from the other party. So, I went to the garage to feed my heart on ire. I pushed the door open rather rudely ... I stood nonplussed, looking at the scene. Granny was sitting on the floor; she was surrounded by a host of kids — four of them my own — listening with rapt attention to a story she was narrating. When she saw me, she smiled mechanically?

'I thought the garage had been vacated.' I said and felt furious with myself for the apologetic undertone in my voice.

'Tell us what happened after that, Nani,' urged my youngest son, clearly indicating that my intrusion was unwelcome. Granny placed an affectionate hand on his shoulder and said to me:

'Pani makes promises in earnest, but he cannot keep them. My daughter-in-law has gone out to look for some buttons. Son, we don't want to cause you any inconvenience; as soon as this saree on which I am working is mended, I will leave.'

She smiled again, and I was strangely affected. I felt that smile enter my innermost being and fill me with a sense of well-being. I turned back, impulsively, trying to fight that feeling which threatened to jeopardise my rights over the garage and the affection of my children. She went on with the narration of her story and her sewing. Pani lit the fire, and when it began to blaze, we adjourned into the shed in the crematorium. It was open on all sides and looked windswept. The masonry pillars were worn out on their southeast corners from years of impact from sand particles driven by the wind. Pani lay down on the cement floor of the shed and broke into his usual drunken monologue: 'Saar, Mother was not really my mother! She was actually my aunt! My mother's younger sister! She was ... what do they call Father's younger wife? She was what they call Father's second wife. But what a mother she was, Saar! How can I live without her? Tell me, Saar, how can I live without her? I had heard the whole story in bits from Granny's own mouth, as she casually mentioned an event here and an event there to my wife and children from time to time. What struck me as unique was her manner of presenting things. The gruesome details sounded like pleasant reminiscences as narrated by her. 'My husband died a little this or that side of my marriage,' she would say and have a good laugh over it. The sum and substance of it was that he had tied the thali around her neck and then went and died in the arms of his concubine. She was left with a lot of property, a lot of debts and an infant three months old, the son of her elder sister, who was her husband's third wife. That girl had died in childbirth, and her parents had wanted to get Granny married to her sister's husband as his fourth wife, mainly on account of the child Pani. Pani grew up a true scion of the Zamindar family. In Granny's words, 'Goddess Lakshmi was a prisoner in our house due to some curse and got her release the day Pani attained his majority.' While a minor, Pani borrowed huge sums of money against the day of attainment of his majority. He had a couple of imported cars and a host of concubines all over the twin Godavari districts. Small wonder, the property disappeared like camphor! By the time he was 20, twelve huge chests of jewels were all that remained, worth about six to seven lakhs of rupees in those days. And those boxes, too, soon became empty one after another.

'Daughter, Granny would tell my wife, 'Do you know what I used to do? When it came to the tenth chest, I started stealing my own jewels and hiding them in odd corners of the house. Actually, the jewels were mine — my mother-in-law's gift to me on the occasion of my marriage. But what could I do? It was the streets for us if the last chest became empty.' When Pani reached the end of his resources, she sold the jewels she had saved and persuaded Pani to invest the money in some venture which would ensure them a steady monthly income. Her elder sister's son was running a prosperous business in Madras, making cardboard boxes. Pani became a partner in that venture, investing in it some fifty thousand rupees. But what was fifty thousand for one who had squandered away fifty lakhs in five years? Her nephew got sick of the partnership when Pani's personal debts far exceeded his assets in the business, and he terminated the arrangement.

But, out of consideration for the family, he appointed Pani as the sole agent of the company. Of course, he did the work himself and paid the commission to Pani. But Pani was not the one to be satisfied with an allowance and proved that he could raise money on 'future' incomes, too! So much so that his cousin had to give a notification in the papers that Pani was no longer their sole agent and that his creditors had no claim on the company. Now he was giving a meagre allowance to the family, and Pani had to switch over to patta from the costly imported drinks he was used to consuming. Of course, Pani was never tired of falling foul of his cousin. 'The skull has broken!' said the purohit, and we all went to the pyre.

`Lakshmikanthamma-Suramma-Peram-maanaam! chanted the purohit, and performed most of the ritual himself, as Pani was in no condition to comprehend his instructions. I couldn't reconcile the same Lakshmi-Kanthamma with Granny. I tried hard to visualize her as a young girl called Lakshmikanthamma sitting bashfully in the ceremonial pandal, clad heavily in the sumptuous finery of a Zamindar's bride. But the picture did not fit. To me, and to everyone who had known her in her last days, she was just Granny, with the veil of the widow and that divine smile lighting up her entire face. As we turned homeward, Pani suddenly ran up and fell on the smouldering pyre, crying, 'Mother, how can I live without you?'

However, promptly we pulled him back: he had sustained a few burns, but he was beyond any physical pain. The alcoholic agony of his loss took violent possession of him, and tears flowed in torrents from his eyes. He had shed drunken tears on many occasions, but these tears now, though out of self-pity, were the only genuine tears he had ever shed. I felt a great pity welling up in my heart for him, probably for the first and last time. I ate like a glutton that noon, and my wife was surprised that I felt a great load had been lifted off my heart. I turned the fan on, full blast, and lay down on the bed. Pani came quiet and preoccupied. I closed my eyes. But Pani knew, with the sure insight of a child, that I was not asleep. After a long pause, he said, 'Granny has gone to heaven! She told me all good people go to heaven!' I opened my eyes and looked at him. There was a smile on his face. It had simple expectancy. But it also had an agedness. Granny had let a little of herself in my children, and I knew that it was for the good of them. My wife had often said that Granny was spoiling the children. But even she, in her heart of hearts, knew that Granny's influence on the children was healthy. She was so completely one of them and yet so far away from them that she commanded their confidence and respect alike. Even my eldest son Babi, who was a little devil by any reckoning, would rather die than offend her. She inculcated in them an unconscious desire to be good in her eyes. But she never prescribed a code of conduct for them, nor did she ever curb their propensity for mischief. It was a sort of goodness which embodied everything they liked to be: mischievous, hilarious, and even riotous. But that goodness had another dimension to it so that she, who was such a great influence on every child, could not mend her own Pani. I pondered over this paradox time and again but could not find a satisfactory answer. One day, Nani drank off half a bottle of kerosene, and my wife beat him in a fit of anxiety and helplessness. Granny snatched the child away from her and literally ran to the doctor, a furlong away.

But for prompt action, Nani's survival would have been difficult. My wife felt miserable that she should have beaten her own ailing child but was too proud to admit it. When Nani's recovery was reasonably certain, she said, 'I wish the mischievous devil were dead. He is taking the life out of me!'

'If anything, untoward had happened to him, you would have been miserable for life!' remarked Granny, 'Can you find such a sweet child anywhere? Of course, he will not drink any more kerosene. He has had a taste of it, and that's enough.' The child was lying in Granny's lap, in a semi-conscious state, following the sedative given by the doctor. He smiled sleepily into Granny's eyes. But my wife could not brook the idea of another woman's siding with her son against her. 'You pet the children too much, Granny! Had you thrashed your Pani when he was this age, he would not have become what he is today!'

In saying this, there was in my wife's voice a note of vicious satisfaction, a satisfaction of having scored a point over Granny. But Granny simply looked at her and smiled. There was a dreamlike haziness in her eyes as she said, 'Perhaps you are right, daughter. You see, I cannot even see and endure physical pain in others. How then could I inflict it? But daughter, I have seen boys, thrashed mercilessly in their childhood by their parents, grow up to be cruel rogues. However, your Nani is a gem. He will become as great a man as Jawaharlal Nehru one day!' From then on, Nani, for his part, had only one ambition: to become a Jawaharlal one day. It altered his entire conduct and made a new boy of him. Neither I nor my wife would have been able to plant that idea so firmly in young Nani's mind. Granny was a great storyteller. She could never describe a character in terms of abstract qualities. She would say, for instance, 'Dharmaraj was just like your father. He would fuss and beat his head and cry when he wanted to have his way. When he sent Abhimanyudu to break the Padmavyuham, did he not know for certain that the boy would be killed? And, when the boy was killed, what did he do? He sat with his hands on his head and wept like a woman. Of course, he loved Abhimanyudu. But he wept because he was afraid of facing Arjuna when he returned that evening. Do you know what our famous Vemanna said about him? He is Dharmaraju only in name; he is a large-sized neem seed.' Thus, I became Dharmaraju, my wife was Kunthi and Pani was Kamsudu or Duryodhannadu, and the sense of identification in the minds of the children was complete. Thanks to Granny, stories from the Puranas and old legends, though far away in space and time, were peopled by men and women the children knew intimately.

Granny and family stayed on in the garage on account of an unforeseen development. A week after

I shifted into the new premises, some engineers and their staff started to measure up the road in front of my home. I learnt from them that a huge over bridge was going to be constructed across the railway line and that the road near my house would rise to a sheer height of over twenty feet. It would take about a year for the road and the over bridge to be completed, and meanwhile, the approach road to my house would be cut off; it would be laid under the new bridge when it was completed. Until then, I would not be able to bring my car to my house. So, it was not worthwhile insisting on Granny and family vacating the garage. I found another garage on the other side of the railway line. Every evening, I would leave the car in that garage and cross over the railway line to my house.

The scaffolding of the new bridge rose steeply, a few feet in front of my house, cutting off the view of the other side completely. As I left my car in the garage and crossed the railway line every evening, the feeling grew that we were being entombed alive. Granny and the children would be sitting on the masonry ledges or on the heaps of rubble, unmindful of the dust and the cement. Sometimes, she would be talking to the workmen in her characteristic Telugu, with its East Godavari drawl. She would advise Muthu on how he could bring round his intransigent young bride or sympathise with Palani for the perfidy of his brother. They talked in Tamil, and she in Telugu, with Babi playing interpreter if the need ever arose. Sometimes, she would narrate to the kids the story of the Ramayana, which would be rendered vivid by the actions of Babi and the other children. Invariably, Babi played the role of Hanuman and jumped from one heap of rubble onto another, demonstrating the famous leap across the ocean for the Sanjeevi hill. My wife used to grumble at the state of the hair and dress of the children, but Granny would range them in the bathroom every evening and wash them clean. The ritual was a riot, lasting about an hour, and the merriment enlivened the entire neighbourhood. A few more cakes of soap were expended in the process, but I was glad that the children were enjoying themselves. One day, Babi, playing Hanuman as usual, jumped on Granny, enacting the killing of Lankini. Granny was then precariously poised on a masonry ledge and was caught unawares. Both of them fell down a height of nearly six feet, but, fortunately, neither was hurt. That night, Granny complained of a little pain in the chest, but none of us thought it was anything serious. As I was having breakfast on the third day of Granny's obsequies, Babi ran in announcing the arrival of Pani's wife, Venkamma, and her children. As we entered the garage, Venkamma, who was sitting reclining against a wall, stood up, and Lakshmi, her eldest daughter, was looking about the garage in the vain hope of finding Granny somewhere. There were no tears in her eyes, but there was a puzzled, anxious look in them. She was Granny's pet. When Pani started to drink away more than half the allowance his cousin gave and left the family to starve for the better part of the month, I had to butt in. It was too much to see a whole family starving when I returned home after a hard day's work. So, I called Pani's cousin, and, between us, we agreed that the allowance should be made over to my wife, who would pay the monthly bills of the family and see that adequate provisions were made available in their house. This, however, did not suit Pani's convenience. One night, we were awakened by terrified shrieks and shouts from the garage and rushed in. Pani's children were running in utter fright, hither and thither, in the yard. Inside the garage, Venkamma was howling, as though she were being lynched. We pushed open the partly closed doors and were confronted by a ghastly sight: Venkamma was lying prone on the ground, and Lakshmi was covering her mother, receiving ceaseless thrashings at the hands of her father. Pani was hitting her with a piece of bamboo in a mad frenzy. Granny was lying bleeding in one corner, evidently unconscious. The devilishness of the whole scene was accentuated for me when I saw Lakshmi not even whimper but beg her mother, in whispers, not to raise her voice.

I snatched the bamboo from Pani's hands and slapped him hard on his right cheek with such force that he collapsed in a corner. I rushed out, shouting that I would ring the police. As I was entering my drawing room, where the phone was, Lakshmi ran up from behind and caught my legs, virtually preventing me from reaching the phone. Shedding tears of anguish, she begged me not to inform the police. I felt deflated and collapsed in a chair. I felt guilty and resentful at the same time. What right had the girl to put me in such an awkward position? I was awed by the picture of her covering her mother and receiving all those vicious thrashings without uttering so much as a whimper. The next day, Granny insisted on Venkamma's going to her father's place with the children. Pani was not particularly fond of his wife, but I think his pride was hurt. He resorted to quite a few tricks to prevent his wife and children from going away. He dashed his head against the wall, threatening to kill himself, slapped his cheeks hard, took vows of good conduct on all the gods of the Hindu pantheon, and finally prostrated himself at the feet of his wife, who instinctively stepped back, horrified at the impropriety of such an action. Thereafter, she did soften a little, but Granny was firm. She told her son, 'Sarmagaru (that's me) gave me an ultimatum — that, if they stayed here, he would call the police. I promised him that I would send them away. Now, be a good boy and do not make things difficult for all of us. After a couple of months, we can convince him and bring them back. It was a deliberate lie, but it served its purpose very effectively. She knew Pani would not have the courage to face me after what had happened the previous night. But Pani also knew, in his heart of hearts, that the parting between him and his wife was more or less final. It became suddenly clear to me that Pani was an overgrown, peevish, self-willed child and that Granny treated him as such. Venkamma, too, knew that the estrangement was complete and felt miserable. She felt prostrate at her mother-in-law's feet and stayed that way for quite some time, trying to control her tears. After they had gone, Granny told my wife, 'It is not so much for the sake of my daughter-in-law that I sent them away! A wife has to make the best of a bad husband. But I shudder to think what would happen to the children if they stayed here. I do not want them to grow up with bitterness and hatred in their hearts.' My respect for Granny grew immensely when I heard her say this. I had come across very few women who were capable of both love and judgement where their own children were concerned. When Venkamma and the children arrived, Pani was fortunately away at the crematorium, collecting Granny's ashes. To avoid any ugly scenes which would mar the dignity and gravity of the occasion, I asked my wife to keep Venkamma and the children in our house and not leave them alone with Pani in the garage. But I was both surprised and gratified to find that Pani was the picture of an ideal head of a bereaved family. After the first burst of tears, he enquired after the welfare of each member of his father-in-law's family. The subsequent days passed off without any incident. In the happy days when she was in our midst, I often used to wonder whether Granny's wisdom and personality would be any good outside the narrow domestic sphere. Would she, for instance, be able to manage things with such ease and confidence if she were placed in such a position as I was? Again, could she reduce the irreconcilable attitudes of labour and management in a big business undertaking such as ours to some sort of a human level? As the personnel officer of our concern, I was often placed in very trying situations when I wondered if I could develop into a granny of big business. My rational mind told me that it was impossible: grannies were no good outside the domestic sphere. But there now came about an interesting episode in which Granny's indirect influence saved me from a very awkward situation. A big strike was in the offing in our factory, and I had to make a momentous decision. I had no doubt that the demands of the labour union were just, both from the legal and the moral standpoint, but as I was an employee of the company, the management expected me to twist the law to suit their viewpoint. I got some hints and threats from high quarters that a wrong step would cost me my job. It became a matter of prestige for the management to stick to their stand and not to yield to the threats of the union. I spent a couple of sleepless nights and ultimately wrote out a note in which I made the actual legal position clear to the management in language as polite as I could manage.

I was asked to present myself before the Board of Directors 'to explain my viewpoint'. When I stepped into their august presence, I felt like a cat on a hot plate, fidgety and nervous.

Their bespectacled looks and tight lips made me feel faint. I suddenly found myself equivocating, and then my mind began to wander, probably to save itself from complete demoralization. The picture of Granny, sitting on the heap of rubble and settling the disputes of workmen with that calm, confident smile, came to my mind. It brought peace to my troubled sensibilities, and, unconsciously, her smile spread over my face. I heard the managing director ask me, quite suddenly, if I was prepared to resign my job on the issue. I was subconsciously aware of having looked into his eyes, smiling like Granny, and saying, simply, 'Yes.'

The entire Board gaped at me for quite some time, but the smile never left my face. They must have been puzzled, not so much by my answer as by the smile. After what seemed like ages, the Managing Director stood up, saying, 'You are a courageous man, Mr Sarma, and an honest one. We are proud of you.' He then shook hands with me with genuine warmth, and I seemed to walk on air as I went out of the room. I left my car in the garage and crossed the railway line. I was eager to see Granny sitting on the heap of rubble, particularly that evening. The sight became such a habit with me that, even on any other evening, I would have been disappointed if I had not seen her there. That evening, my heart literally missed a beat when I found that neither she nor the children were there. I went and first looked in the garage. The garage was pulsating with young life: Granny was reclining on the floor and narrating to the kids the story of the dog that followed Dharmaraju to heaven. She tried to sit up when she saw me, but she was in obvious pain. The smile was, however, there when she answered my enquiries about her health. She told me that it was just the same old pain in the chest. I suggested calling in a doctor, but she said it was not necessary. That night, around 3 a.m., Pani's drunken shouts woke us up. My wife and I went to see what was the matter. We heard Pani shout, at the top of his voice, 'Raise it still higher, I'm dying, you old fool! `Don't shout! You'll wake up everyone in the neighbourhood.'

Granny was remonstrating. Her voice showed intense physical strain. I cautioned my wife to be silent and approached the garage. I peeped in through the slit between the double doors. It was dark inside. I flashed my torch through the gap, and the sight all but struck me dumb. Pani was lying on the heavy wooden cot, and he was urging Granny to lift the hind side of the cot still higher. Granny stood there, bearing the weight of the cot on her bent back, trying to support her buckling knees with her hands. I pushed open the door with a violent jerk of my shoulders and switched on the light. Granny saw us and smiled automatically. She tried to free herself, lowering the cot, but her legs were too stiff to bend. I ran forward to take the burden off her back, but, before I could reach her, she lurched forward and fell down, vomiting blood. My wife ran up to her, calling, 'Granny, Granny!' Pani sat up, not knowing what had knocked him into temporary consciousness. He saw me and said, half apologetically, 'You see, Saar, the fumes clear when the blood flows into the head. The hind side of the cot must be lifted high. The higher it is lifted, the more comfortable

I feel!' I felt nauseated at this and turned my face away. Granny must have been bearing this terrible burden of a drunken son for ages on her bent back. The long nights must have stretched into eternities of torture. She had the capacity to conceal within herself all the unexpected sorrows of her existence — without a complaint, without expecting solace — and give to everyone else that smile which lit up their hearts. What was she if not Shiva, who drank up the all-annihilating poison and left the life-giving nectar for others to enjoy! I found myself weeping like a child; I am not sure if it was sorrow that filled my heart. 'What is the good of crying? Hurry up and bring a doctor, said my wife. I hurried away and brought a doctor, but Granny did not need the service of a doctor any more. She had found her escape from a burden she had borne too long .... From Pani's general behaviour after his wife and children returned, I concluded that he had really turned over a new leaf. I thought the loss of his mother had sobered him and hoped he would, from this point at least, shoulder the responsibility of looking after his family. So, I was taken aback when young Lakshmi came and told us, on the thirteenth day after Granny's death, that her mother and children would be going back to her grandfather's place that very evening. I asked her if her father was accompanying them. She replied, 'My mother would die the same way as Granny if she lived with Father. Then who will look after the children? Granny told my mother, specifically, never to yield to his entreaties and go and live with him. He has no control over himself. I smiled, wryly, to myself because she did not seem to include herself as one among the children. Cabs were off the road that day on account of a general taxi strike sparked off by some dispute between one of the drivers and a police constable. So, I had to drive the family to the central station that evening.

My wife and children too came to see them off; we might not see them again for a long time. After they got into the train, my wife gave a five-rupee note to each one of the children, including Lakshmi. Venkamma protested mildly, and the children hesitated a little when my wife explained there was no delicacy involved, that we lived as one family and the bond that Granny had forged between us need not die with her.

My wife stood talking to Venkamma near a window of the compartment, and Pani was at another window, carrying on a conversation in whispers with young Lakshmi. I stood a little distance away from the compartment, my mind idling. The departure of the train was announced, and we had hurriedly got the children out, seated as they were with Pani's children in the compartment. As I was helping Pani down the crowded doorway, I saw Lakshmi surreptitiously put the five-rupee note that my wife had given her in Pani's palm and close his fingers over it, lest anyone notice it. I also heard her whisper, 'Don't spend all of it tonight. If you spend it away today, who will give you tomorrow?' `I won't! I won't!' Pani was saying, his voice choked with emotion. As the train started to move, I saw her smile. Her eyes were wet with something more divine than tears, and her face had the radiance of sunshine after rain. I had the sudden illusion that Granny had come to life. At that moment, I had a conviction (the conviction came to me) that resurrection was a fact: this tender girl of ten had already taken upon herself the task of bearing the cross of her father's sins. I felt depressed and elated at the same time.

The famous English adage about their king came to my mind, and I said to myself:

'Granny is dead; long live Granny!'

> Translated by Shri Palagummi Padmaraju
> (Rendered from the original story in Telugu)
> Published in Modern Indian Short Stories by
> Mr.Suresh Kohli - 1974

CHAPTER X

A Bird in Hand

The reverberation of the train wheels moving is faintly heard. Then I realise that the glass doors are closed. I immediately open them. A strong hot breeze and coal dust rush in and invade the compartment. Travelling in a compartment alone in the middle of a scorching summer is a foolish idea; if the glass doors are lowered, it's noisy, and if lifted, it's the hot air. Even when it got dark, the air didn't cool down.

Moreover, one should never travel alone in a coupe. There should be someone to accompany you. As age advances, desires increase.

Nostalgia hit me as I recalled my honeymoon trip. It was summer then too, but those days were different. It was on the second day after my marriage that my wife and I travelled to Bengaluru. I didn't even think about buying the ticket in advance or reserving the berths. However, I secretly got my wife into a taxi, informing my mother alone as a hint. Behind us, my brother-in-law chased us in another taxi. He caught us on Mount Road. He handed my wife a suitcase packed with saris and gave me some money too, patting my shoulder before leaving.

While I was wandering anxiously on the platform, Parameshwara Rao greeted me. He asked, "Who are you, and where are you headed?" Perhaps he had seen me pleading with the reservation inspector. His uniform and the lamp in his hand spoke loudly that he was a guard. That was the first interaction with him. Later, he became a close friend. Parameshwara Rao is a great man. He set both of us into a compartment, along with our luggage. We shut all the doors. Then, there was no discomfort, no boredom, no hunger, and no sleep. Late at night, around ten or eleven, Parameshwara Rao knocked on the door.

"You seem to be in a state of wondering whether you're hungry or not; I won't let you get away with protests," he said. A young man who accompanied him brought a tiffin carrier for us and placed it in the coupe. Until we started eating, we didn't realise how hungry we were. I was overwhelmed by his warmth and hospitality.

In that crazy enthusiasm, one tends to forget everything: the summer heat, the noise, and the irritation. But now that enthusiasm has faded. As age advances, the mind drifts away from the cool breezes under the moonlight. When the mind has that coolness akin to the moonlight, what does it matter if it's not there outside? When a person gets restless and irritated about the outside atmosphere, it means he has already attained old age.

Maybe it is Sullurupeta; for some reason, the train halted. I opened the door. "Hello, Mr Ramanujulu! Unexpectedly we meet," said a gentleman as he boarded the compartment.

"Come, come," I said. I couldn't recall who he was.

His face looked familiar from somewhere. From where? He looked like a decent gentleman. Whoever he might be, he'd keep me company. Sharing this noise with someone is much better than experiencing it all alone. I should engage him in conversation and find out his whereabouts. How could I forget such a friendly face? What better sign than ageing?

"How far?"

"I can't say. Maybe until Vijayawada. If necessary, Waltair."

Oh my God! Where do I place him in four districts? It wouldn't be polite if I asked him, "Who are you, sir? I can't remember." How long can I prolong this conversation?

"What are you doing now?"

"Oh, the usual."

This conversation is not getting anywhere. If only his answers had the names of mutual friends, it could lead to some connection.

"You haven't been coming to the club lately—our Ramineedu is the secretary now, are you aware?" I ventured.

"No," was the reply.

What does he not know? Doesn't he know Ramineedu? Or doesn't he know that he's become the secretary? Come what may, I was prompted to ask another question.

"How are your children doing?"

"All children are my children. You know my vow of Brahmacharya, and you understand my dedication to it, don't you?" He laughed, "Ha-Ha-Ha."

His laughter mocked me, blending with the noise of the train. Even after his laughter stopped, it resonated in my mind. Fortunately, Govindu came from Sullurupeta, reminding me of the food I had packed. I decided to leave this man alone, have my meal, and get some sleep. Still, as a matter of courtesy, I asked, "Please come; let's share a meal."

"I don't eat at night," he replied.

Alright, if I don't know who he is, what loss is it to me? If need be, he will state it himself. Why should I bother? However, if he, whom I barely know, mentions his town and name, what's the harm? Why should he pester me like a fly wriggling in phlegm?

The meal wasn't good. The yoghurt was sour. After closing the tiffin box, I went and washed my hands.

I should have asked Ranga Rao to sit in this compartment. We could kill time chatting. But how would he come if I hadn't invited him? In these government jobs, the difference in grades cannot be forgotten either by small executives or their superiors. I am the superintendent, and he is the circle inspector. Tomorrow, if he becomes the superintendent, he will keep the circle inspectors at arm's length. I consider this a personal issue. In reality, in what way is Ranga Rao any less in comparison to the person sitting next to me? Doesn't he perceive me as an equal or just another person? Finding out his name would be ideal.

"Would you like a cigarette, Mister...?" I extended, hoping he might fill in the blanks for me.

"I don't smoke," he replied frankly.

"Since when did you stop, Mr Subbarao?" I casually asked.

"It's been a long time."

Then, this man's name is Subbarao. In Andhra Pradesh, half the population are Subbaraos. It would be good if the government announced a law that no one could name their children Subbarao anymore. Subbarao has become synonymous with a man in Telugu land. I suppose there are Subbaraos in Karnataka too. Is he an acquaintance from Bengaluru during my stay there years ago?

The face, though, seems familiar.

"By the way, Mr Subbarao..."

"My name's Ramarao."

"Oh, Mr Ramarao!"

Oh God, when I earlier called him Subbarao, why did he remain silent? So, his name is Ramarao, but what's the use? In Andhra Pradesh, half of them are Subbaraos, while the other half are Ramaraos.

It feels like a dead end! Why should I care at this age? I lay down and closed my eyes. I shifted my thoughts toward Sridhar.

Sridhar was found, but he immediately slipped off like mercury. It's Ranga Rao's mistake; once the person was caught, why didn't he disclose it to me? Was he basking in the glory of finding him all by himself? Actually, no, that's unjust of me to think that way; Ranga Rao had no one to help him. Suddenly, Sridhar appeared. He acted like an old friend and took him to his place. Sridhar's heart is cold. In broad daylight, in full view of ten people, he entered the bank, frightened the cashier, and ran away with ten thousand rupees. Hence, once a man is caught, that's it. There are ten witnesses to prove the case. Poor Ranga Rao... he caught him! But Sridhar was very smart. He told Ranga Rao that he had to go to the toilet and then escaped from there. Fortunately, the central traffic police spotted him. So exiting from the station is impossible. He could board trains only. Kolkata Mail, Bombay Mail, Bengaluru Mail – where will he go? Where could he escape now? All trains are being searched thoroughly. The blame is solely on Ranga Rao. Would someone with so much experience let the fool go? Fine, what is the point of worrying over spilt milk? Poor Ranga Rao seems to be embarrassed. That's why he didn't agree to travel with me in this compartment. I need to coax him. After all, people do make mistakes.

"Mr Ramanujachari, are you sleeping?" asked the man.

"Don't be in a hurry. I'll rest after we cross Guduru."

Does he even know who I am? He knows my name. If he knew anything more, wouldn't it come out in the conversation? Is he, like me, wrapped in confusion? Is he trying to remember where we met or our mutual friends?

Oh God! My mind felt lighter. He and I are in the same boat. Ha, ha, ha… What a strange situation! Now we can talk comfortably. A name known to both of us anywhere will resolve the dilemma on each side.

"Ramarao! What a wonderful poker game Tiruvengadam played the other day!", I said.

"Really?" he said hesitantly. Looks like he doesn't know Tiruvengadam. Great! This is exciting. Time will pass splendidly from now on. Moreover, shouldn't I take revenge for the trouble he's caused me all this while?"

Each break felt nothing less than a hundred. He hit four or five hundred so easily."

"Oh!"

Why does he respond so casually? How peculiar is the mind? This Ramarao shifts dramatically, sometimes being Mister, sometimes him, and sometimes someone else, with no respect at all, depending on the mindset.

"Have you seen the movie The Thief? There's not a single dialogue. It's done brilliantly."

"I haven't seen it," he replied casually. Why does he look so lost suddenly?

Oh! How stuffy it has become in the compartment. Looks like we've reached Guduru. The speed is reducing. I opened the door and stood at the doorway. I stepped down as the train halted. Ranga Rao was coming from a distance towards my compartment. Oh God, it feels like life has returned. Ranga Rao has arrived, and we are chatting away as we walk. Ranga Rao said:

"We searched all compartments. We examined every person intensely. There's nobody on this train."

"Did he board this train at all?"

"Yes, he boarded this train. Because our head constable got on one side of the sleeper compartment, and Sridhar got off on the other side."

"Where?"

"In Sullurupeta."

"Oh! Then, we should have conducted a search operation there; we could have caught him easily?"

"Yes, that's the mistake he made; he didn't inform me. He led the operation himself. He made one constable enter every compartment and conduct a search. He even checked the train from the start to the end while the train was moving."

"Then he must have slipped away in Sullurupeta itself. What's the use of travelling on this train now?"

"Exactly," Ranga Rao responded. "The head is making calls to all stations here. They have tightened the security to catch Sridhar, especially at the Sullurupeta railway station; I have personally sent the news to the station."

"How will we reach Madras?"

"I have a friend here. I sent a note with a constable asking him to send his car."

I returned to the compartment. Ramarao was lying on the upper berth. I started folding my holdall, and he asked,

"What's up, sir? Are you getting down?"

"I think the plan has gone awry," I said.

Why should I tell him my story? Who am I? What's my job? Why am I getting down in the middle of the journey? Let him break his head and die of curiosity! He killed me for four hours, wondering about him, and now it's his turn.

"You can use my berth," I said a little sarcastically.

"Thank you," he said.

Meanwhile, Govindu arrived.

"Govindu! There should be soap and a towel in the bathroom; please check, and put those two books in the small box. Don't forget the water bottle."

By the time Govindu finished unloading, Ranga Rao arrived.

"Hey Ranga Rao, did you unload your bags?"

"I did, sir."

"Excuse me, Ramarao!" I said while getting ready to descend. As I was about to step down, Ramarao stood behind me to close the door. Ranga Rao stood frozen, staring at something behind me as if he saw a ghost.

Ranga Rao suddenly blew the whistle. The moving train stopped with a creak. "What are you looking at? Let me get down; the train is moving," I said. Ranga Rao ran towards the compartment. I jumped down with a little irritation.

"Come from that side; he got off over there. It is him, Sridhar. He slipped through the goods compartment. Hurry, catch him!" shouted Ranga Rao.

"Where's Sridhar?" I asked anxiously. "It's him, the one who travelled in your compartment; as soon as he saw me, he got down from the other side. You were covering him, Sir, otherwise..." Before he finished, Ranga Rao ran off.

Oh my God! That's Sridhar's face; I've seen it in a photo! Did he recognise me? How did he board without knowing me? He definitely knows me! But how the hell did he find out my name? Oh! The reservation charts! What a fool I was! How did I forget the first rule of police training—that you should compare every face to the one you've seen in the photo? Why didn't that thought ever cross my mind?

Moreover, I let go of the bird in hand. I also blamed Ranga Rao for his foolishness. What a mess I created! How foolish am I? A bird in hand! Once it slips away, will I ever be able to catch it again?

Oh... A bird in hand!

- Translated by Ms. Palagummi Seetha
(Daughter of Shri Palagummi Padmaraju)
(Rendered from the original story Chethiki Chikkina
Pitta written by Palagummi Padmaraju in Telugu)

CHAPTER XI

The Man and the Maid

Professor Ramagopal was too debonair and suave for the dull and humble calling of a teacher of chemistry in a small college. He heartily disliked the honorific prefix 'Professor', which some of his friends and colleagues persisted in using, in spite of many remonstrances on his part. The word was associated in his mind with a horrible statue in Blackstone, severe in outline, inhuman in its aspect, signifying bearing dissociated completely from the context of the human being and culture petrified once and for all. He was natural by instinct and artificial by design, and the change from one attitude to another was so quick and natural that people put it down to a natural perversity in him.

In the company of male friends, he behaved with complete abandon, ate his food with the relish of a bohemian, cut jokes with strangers and also enjoyed an occasional joke at himself with absolute good humour. But he became stiff and artificial in the company of women, always trying to make an impression on them, though he wore the veil that usually lapsed into a polite and apologetic discourse about the natural dullness of the female mind compared to that of the male. But the ladies considered him interesting because they never took him seriously. His friends and colleagues thought him charming, and the authorities of the college tolerated him for all his unorthodox views, putting their faith in the age-old proverb that a barking dog could never bring itself to bite.

There was one circumstance which was responsible for Ramagopal's popularity all round. He was twenty-five and unmarried. He successfully dodged the attempts of numerous prospective fathers-in-law and thus became the exception that proved the general rule that no eligible young man in this country could long remain unmarried beyond the age of twenty. So, the events leading up to his dismissal from the college took everybody by surprise, including Ramagopal himself.

He became suddenly conscious of those innocent eyes while he was teaching one day the laws of chemical combinations to his class. He was making an impressive lecture expatiating on the natural affinity between two things very dissimilar to each other, drawing profuse analogies from nature, when his mind lost its thread, arrested by something in those eyes. They were looking straight and unblinking at his face, concentrating on some point behind him which he could not derive.

He was irritated and immediately flung a question at the owner of those eyes.

"What was I saying just now?"

The girl stood up embarrassed and said, "I am sorry, sir, I was not listening to you."

There were tears in her eyes, probably occasioned by her discomfiture in the open class, and Ramagopal momentarily regretted having asked her that question. The rest of the hour, he somehow pulled on, not being able to recapture his former expansive mood. Those eyes haunted him for long hours after the class was over. Though he was familiar with the faces of his students, he generally did not remember their names. So, he made a particular note of the name of the girl, 'Radha', while he was marking the attendance in the practical class. During the two hours he was conducting the practical class, he observed her closely and was charmed with the dexterity and neatness of her method of working. When she came to him with her observation notebook, he said, looking into it, "You girls can no doubt write up the record very neatly, but I wonder, do you ever think of becoming students of science? Science requires a male mind to master it." Radha replied, "Are there not many ladies who achieved distinction in sciences, Sir? For instance, Madame Curie." Ramagopal laughed and said, "That is an exception." The conversation was cut short by an exclamation of Radha.

When Ramagopal looked down, he saw Radha's pen on the ground and quite a sprinkling of the ink on his trousers.

Radha apologised profusely for her inadvertence. Ramagopal made light of it, but he carried a strong suspicion in his mind that the dropping of the pen was not accidental. Thus began a series of events which looked quite innocent but which confirmed some suspicions in the mind of Ramagopal. He could not put his finger on any point and prove to even himself the truth of what he suspected. In her movements, in her eyes and cheeks, and in the subtle shades of her voice when she addressed him, he felt that there was something not quite so innocent as others might think. Sometimes she jostled with him as if by chance in the narrow passages between the laboratory tables.

Sometimes, she came to him with very silly doubts and artlessly touched his hands while taking back her record book from him. Ramagopal, though he was sure he was the master of his own emotions, was all the while conscious of her movements when she was in his presence, and thoughts of her filled him when she was not. Of course, he told himself that he was just enjoying a big joke all the while.

The event which confirmed his suspicions beyond any possible doubt happened when he led an excursion of his students to the Papi Hills. He, along with a number of boys, was bathing in the Godavari, and the girls were watching them from a cliff projecting into the river. Suddenly he heard a yell and a thud, and when he turned, he found a girl had fallen into the river just a few yards from where he was bathing. He swam there in all haste and found that the girl was Radha. She was unconscious, and he had to carry her ashore on his shoulders. As he was going towards the shore, he felt one of her arms circling round his neck, and he felt that the movement was not as unconscious as it looked.

The final event took place one night while he was crossing a garden to reach the main road after a ceremonial function in the college. He waited till all the guests and ladies went away, gave some instructions to the servants with regard to the pulling down of the dais, and then started on his way home by the shortcut across the garden, thinking about the function. He suddenly jostled into another human form in the darkness, and he heard Radha's voice saying, "Sorry, sir." A thousand ideas rushed into his heated brain, and the prominent among them was that Radha was there on the footpath in the garden after all the guests and ladies had left. What was she doing there? Ramagopal completely lost his head at that moment and impulsively caught her in an embrace. There was a terrified shriek from Radha's mouth, and next, Ramagopal was conscious of a battery light being focused on his face, revealing him in a compromising position. As soon as his grip loosened, Radha ran out weeping, and a few girls going ahead of them took charge of her. A cold sweat broke out on the forehead of Ramagopal.

The next day, the principal called him to his room. He had an irritating way of omitting the crucial words when he had to convey anything unpleasant. He said, "You see, we are sorry for what happened, and we are forced to do this." Ramagopal, after some hesitation, said,

"My intentions are honourable, sir."

The principal quickly added.

"No. No. Let us not discuss that aspect of the question. You see, it is inevitable under the circumstances....". He never completed that sentence.

After his dismissal from the college, Ramagopal did not feel like seeking employment in another college. This incident would be given enough publicity, and he did not like to face a sly and hostile world. He was too proud to smart under a defeat at the hands of a chip of a girl and finally decided to conquer the world, especially the world of women, by becoming a writer. He gave up the idea of getting married once and for all and began to equip himself by extensive reading with knowledge of sex and feminine psychology.

Very soon he won recognition as a powerful writer on sex problems. He became especially famous for his analysis of the female mind. There was not one aspect of the devious ways in which the mind of a woman worked in the setup of civilised society that did not come under the searchlight of his analysis. What lent charm to his writings was a peculiar condescending attitude towards women tinged with an assumed sympathy and understanding. His popularity among the ladies of high society was unprecedented. He was always in demand at women's clubs, dinner parties and even family gatherings.

There were quite a few women who shamelessly hung on to him on those occasions, trying to make an impression. But he remained impervious to all their charms and was secretly pleased with the power he was exercising over them. Ramagopal grew to a ripe old age in all this glory with not a single regret. His writings brought him fame and money.

One day, a gentleman about his own age invited him for dinner at his house. Incidentally, the gentleman added that his wife was a student of Ramagopal when he was a lecturer in chemistry. Ramagopal was intrigued by this circumstance and accepted the invitation. To his utter surprise he found the housewife to be Radha. She greeted him very naturally without any self-consciousness. She was now a mother of several children, and the husband had unqualified faith in his wife and also regard for her. He was very prosaic and practical in his approach to life. After the dinner, the husband said quite casually,

"My wife told me about your initial infatuation for her. And she also claims that she was instrumental in making you what you are."

Ramagopal had an itch to retort, saying that there are things which he could reveal about Radha, but in the meantime, her husband was called away by a superior officer. While going, the husband requested Ramagopal not to go away till he returned. Radha put all the children to bed and sat in the parlour with Ramagopal. She told him that her husband was an income tax officer, and the talk went on about insignificant things for some time. Ramagopal suddenly asked,

"Why did you tell your husband that I was infatuated with you?"

Radha innocently said, "Then, was it not true?"

Ramagopal, looking at those innocent eyes, was puzzled for the first time in several years. He slowly said, "Then why did you shriek like that?" Radha said, "Oh! I was terrified. I thought you would do something terrible."

Ramagopal said, "Then why did you lead me on?" Radha replied, "Did I? ... I have read all your writings. I think what you write about women is all nonsense." Ramagopal was intrigued and said, "Is it?"

Radha went on, "You were entirely mistaken."After a moment she added, "I wept and wept that night. I thought you would have the common decency to go to my father after the event and tell him that you were prepared to marry me to make amends for your conduct." Ramagopal suddenly felt a spasm coursing through him.

He looked at her eyes, which had that innocent look in them after all these years. She was looking at the lamp, lost in her own reminiscences. He sensed something like moisture in them. He instinctively sat up in his chair, and a deep regret of having wasted a lifetime came upon him, and tenderly he asked her, "Radha. Are you happy?"

She looked at him curiously, and there appeared in her eyes a gleam which might be mockery. She broke out into peals of laughter and said, "My husband is one in a million."

Ramagopal felt his gorge rising. He got up and walked away from the house, leaving a surprised Radha, not waiting for her husband to return.

On the way, he felt like a fool, and a terrible depression enveloped him. He resolved never to write any more about women. He felt certain that he did not know anything about them that really mattered.

Translated by Shri Palagummi Padmaraju
(Rendered from the original story Moga Purushudu
Aada Sthri in Telugu)

CHAPTER XII

The Rivals

The Godavari was in spate. The turbid waters, swirling in smoke-like rings, were terrifying even to the bravest. Washermen, however, are undaunted; they swim into midstream to salvage trees and branches and bring them to the bank. By day-break they enter the river. By sundown, the bank is full of twigs and sticks. While the men dare into the midstream, the womenfolk, from the side-lines, try to pull the wood pieces afloat with the aid of hooked poles. The Godavari was quite a stir during those times. While the swollen river uproots whole forests and takes them along its current, men try to obstruct it and collect all those pieces on the bank. Man, thus, retains his mastery over nature.

Collecting them thus requires a lot of skill, not merely strength. When you catch hold of a tree in midstream, you can't control it unless you let yourself be controlled by the stream. There is a challenge in this art, which is a yardstick of the washermen's skill. It is not only the greed for firewood that goads them on, but honour in the game. The winner here is a hero. So, they risk their lives even against the whirlpools.

Rami is a notoriously tough girl. A tiff on everything with everyone comes naturally to her. Under the twilight of dawn, she sets out for the riverside with a hooked pole. Which means that none can approach that part of the river for the day. If anyone dares, well, it is but an invitation to a quarrel. For she has a sharp tongue. Twice or thrice, the police tried to threaten her, but they gave up when she exploded, as was her wont. She would, of course, grant that she didn't own the river or the trees. But no lawyer was able to convince her of the right of other people to encroach on an area which she was the first to occupy. Whatever the question of right and wrong, more people were scared of her tongue, and no woman dared to approach her part of the riverside.

Venkadu is quite a jolly fellow. He can easily pick up a quarrel. He is the hot favourite of all the grown-up girls in the dhobi hamlet. He is a hero in their eyes. There has been some enmity between his father and Rami for a long time now. Venkadu's father had even set fire to Rami's house once.

The mere sight of Venkadu was enough for Rami to start cursing him. But he never bothered himself too much about it because of his innate chivalry. All the girls, however, were allergic to Rami, whom they called a "tomboy".

Venkadu came to know that Rami had been scaring away all the womenfolk from the riverside. One day he went there to see the situation for himself. Rami was busy collecting the twigs. Two or three women were standing by on the bank, eyeing her enviously. Venkadu took a hooked pole into his hands.

Rami, at once, flared up: "You scamp! Come to compete with a woman?"

Venkadu: You ... a woman? Not that I know of... Watch your words, or else you and your hook will be in midstream.

Rami: Why have you come to a place which I had occupied first?

No shame?

Venkadu: Is the riverside your father's property?

Rami: I came first.

Venkadu: I came next.

Rami: Impudent rascal...crossing swords with a woman...

Venkadu: If you promise to be just and quiet. I shall leave.

Rami: Quiet, my foot! I will pick up all my twigs.

Venkadu: O.K.! Those beyond your reach ... let me take.

Rami: Beyond my reach, only in midstream!

Venkadu wouldn't admit defeat by leaving the place. He threw his raft on the bank and began to pull at the twigs with the hook. Venkadu was at a loss to find out how to subdue her. All the other girls of her age would readily succumb to his wink. She alone seemed defiant. Despite the family feud, he never openly offended her. Nor any others, for that matter. But he must now subdue her, somehow.

It was Rami who surpassed Venkadu in collecting twigs from the bank. He watched her skill and grace in the act. Half of the sticks that touched his hook slipped away into the stream. Any stick that touched hers was sure to reach the bank. However much he tried, many of them escaped his grasp. It never struck him that so many of them could be collected from the bank. He sat there in amazed admiration of her expertise.

That day, the Godavari was very fierce. Dark clouds enveloped the sky on all the sides. Slight drizzle with strong winds, many of the washermen were afraid to get into the river that day.

Venkadu, however, chose to enter the river with the raft under his chest. He didn't feel like sitting on the bank, competing with a woman. He dared to enter because few others were ready to do it. Some followed him. He was pushing all his sticks to Rami's side. And she was catching hold of them with determination. By the afternoon, all the others had left, and Rami and Venkadu were left alone. Though he was very tired, Venkadu did not want to leave before Rami.

It was getting dark, the drizzles heavier, and the winds stronger.

"How much longer will you stay?"

"How much longer will you stay?"

Venkadu was about to enter the water again. Rami stood gracefully on the stones on the bank, pulling at the twigs.

"Be careful! You might slip into the waters!"

"Take care of yourself; you needn't pull me out, if I slip in."

"Brave talk; if you were to slip in, I alone will have to pull you out."

As a big tree floated ahead, Venkadu swam in towards it. The tree was very heavy, and he was very tired. He wouldn't have jumped in, but for the rivalry with Rami. He somehow got hold of the tree and was slowly moving towards the bank. He looked up towards the bank; it was all dark. Struggling slowly, he could see it faintly.

Up to her waist in the water, Rami was trying hard to hook a heavy branch.

"It's pretty difficult; leave it alone," he shouted at her. "You better look after your own tree," she retorted.

What is she to him? The obstinate wretch – doesn't she know? She gets in deeper, only to die. But he couldn't help looking towards the bank. Rami staggered once and steadied herself. Venkadu suppressed a shout, and trying not to look that side, was swimming towards the bank.

Meanwhile, there was a sound of something slipping down. His heart sank, and his hands left the tree. He looked up, and Rami wasn't there. He swam towards the bank as fast as he could. Ten yards downstream he could see a head swirling. He lifted Rami up with one hand. She clung to his neck with both her hands. Both of them sank, but he freed himself with difficulty and was able to float and breathe. Rami became unconscious. He slowly placed her neck on his and steadied himself with the other hand. The current then pushed them both away from the bank. He was wondering if he could reach the bank. His hands were becoming unsure and his breath unsteady. Eyes shut; he was dragging the two bodies towards the bank. It was like an age by the time his hand felt the bank, where it was sharply cut by the stream. With a great effort he raised his hand and placed it on the bank. A lump of earth gave way, and both of them sank again. He was about to pass out. Somehow, slowly he carried both the bodies to the bank. He lay supine for a time to regain his breath.

Rami's body stirred. There was a faint moan. He got up and turned her this way and that. In her subconscious state, she held his hand. In that touch of hers she seemed to say a lot, and he seemed to understand it all. Lifting Rami to his shoulders, Venkadu set out for the washerman's hamlet.

Strange to think!

She obviously realised that he had rescued her. He had said that in so many words. And now, it has come to pass.

He had a rivalry with her. How did it arise? Why did he hate her all these days? If she was arrogant, why should he bother? He was bent upon subduing her but failed. That was the cause of his chagrin. No girl was a match to her in catching twigs. She was a true girl. A trifle stubborn, of course; so what? Is he not stubborn himself?

She slipped into the water, and he rescued her. He never did such a noble deed before. This time, she was subdued by him somehow. He thought that he had a moral right over her body, which he had saved after a struggle. He felt he had conquered her. He saw in her a grace, a smoothness and a softness that could be found in no other girl in the world.

When she came to somewhat, she pressed his hand in both hers. There were many things in that touch – gratitude for saving her, admission of defeat in the wager...

Gently putting her down, Venkadu called out to her parents. A large crowd gathered around them. Rami's mother began to beat her breast, crying hysterically. Her father collapsed to the floor, dumbfounded.

The caste elders present were trying to revive her – some pressing the water out, others warming her by a slow fire.

Rami's mother began to wail aloud, "The son of a bitch has killed my darling daughter!" Venkadu was not hearing this wail. His tired eyes were on Rami.

As Rami stirred a little, opening her eyes halfway, Venkadu approached her. He alone was able to see the warmth in her pain-distorted looks. His heart missed a beat. These looks only confirmed the suspicion of Rami's mother. She began to cry louder, "The son of a bitch! He's killed my darling when no one is around!"

Venkadu stood aghast. Was this the reward for all his labours? Rami began to breathe hard. Her father remembered all the old scores with Venkadu.

"I'll fix you; I'll call the police," he said, leaving the place in a huff.

Had he been more tired, Venkadu would have been drowned in the Godavari, along with Rami. He had rescued her, after a great struggle, but to no effect, it seemed. Only the suspicion of a crime remained.

The whole world appeared wicked to Venkadu, in which he and Rami seemed out of place.

- Translated by Dr. D. Anjaneyulu
(Rendered from the original story Pantham written in
Telugu by Palagummi Padmaraju)
Published in Triveni magazine – 1984

CHAPTER XIII

Far Faraway

Banaras to Delhi, Delhi to Madras. Too long a distance even by air. Time does not move. The plane crawls slowly, like a bullock cart. Down below, the hills, rivers, and forests retreat at a leisurely pace.

"We're so close to each other yet leagues apart."

Two lines from scraps of verse Raja had scribbled when he felt like it. There were numberless fleeting moments when I and Raja were together and aeons when we were leagues apart physically and mentally.

Now, Raja's body is awaiting my return to the house, the house we had planned and built together after prolonged sessions of consultations, bickerings, agreements, and exhibitions of temper, a house we longed to possess. The body is now preserved in dry ice, so says the elaborate telegram of Dr Natarajan. Suddenly the air in the plane becomes stifling hot. I feel choked; pull out the paper fan from the back of the front seat. But hands refuse to obey the orders of the brain. Sweat must have appeared on my face. The air hostess bends over the gentleman sitting beside the gangway; I'm in the middle seat next to him – and asks, 'Are you unwell?' 'Water', I ask. She hastens away on unsteady feet as though drunk. The gentleman sitting beside me – past middle age – with all his manly chivalry, comes to the rescue of the damsel in distress, "Don't worry." The first time you travel by plane, you feel dizzy. Walt. I've got a pill; he lifts his briefcase onto his knees and opens it.

The first time you travel by plane, I feel like laughing. But laughter dies in my throat. Several times Raja took me in his trainer plane, put my seatbelt on, and indulged in quite a few acrobatics several times. He was then a pilot trainer in Allahabad, and I was a student of the Banaras Hindu University some ten or twelve years ago.

I refused the pill and sipped the water brought by the hostess. I thanked her. She goes back swaying as though drunk.

That day I was returning home for the vacation. I boarded the plane at Delhi. Just like now, I was sitting in the middle seat of the three on the right side of the gangway. I put on the seatbelt for the take-off. The seat beside the gangway was vacant. Raja came and sat in it, saying, 'Hope you don't mind'. Even before I could answer, he smiled as though he knew I had no objection. Even after the seatbelt sign was put off, he didn't get up. He was talking all through the journey. He was Raja, the 'famous trainer' in the pilot training centre at Allahabad. Could fly three different kinds of aircraft. Had 150 hours of flying experience on each kind. He gave me his Allahabad address, also his Madras address. After we reached Madras, he took my baggage check, almost by force, collected my baggage, and as I was calling a taxi, took me by my arm and got me into the airport van along with the hostesses and traffic staff. I was annoyed at the liberties he had been taking and felt a nameless anxiety; perhaps I liked this encounter. Maybe I felt a little proud, too.

He sat beside me in the airport van. Then he threw it at me, like a thunderbolt out of a clear sky. He sat in the plane beside me with a design. He knew I was studying in Banaras, knew my father and knew my background. He wanted to preface his approach by saying I was lovely. He felt it was too childish an approach and gave it up. He liked me. 'Love at first sight' might sound amateurish, so he didn't say it. As I was getting down from the van, I thought he was a chatterbox, or was he childlike? A fellow who talked like that with a girl on his first acquaintance – what kind of man was he? Maybe he was an old hand at this game, just a philanderer. But was I doing him an injustice? Anyway, why should I encourage a fellow with all those man airs? He would come to my house again on some pretext or other. Then I would give him a piece of my mind.

But he didn't come. Not only the next day but till the end of my vacation. I was looking for him on the beach, in shops, and in restaurants with the sole intention of giving him a piece of my mind, with annoyance that he didn't turn up, with a kind of longing, and with anger that he had cheated me. I spent the entire vacation waiting for him till the day of my return to Banaras, till I entered the huge concentration camp euphemistically called our hostel, with its twelve-foot-high walls and the forbidding matron. When I knew he would not turn up, I felt relieved, almost vacant; vacant, but at peace.

Life fell into the dull routine of going to the classes, returning to the room, roaming about the campus in the company of other girls, commenting about boys, and now and then a visit to the picture house.

And then the exams.

And then he came. I was just showing off to the other girls. I had done exceedingly well in the second English paper. As I entered the hall, the servant told me that the matron wanted me; she was in the visitor's hall. Some relation of mine had come to see me. I wondered who the relation was who came without as much as a letter informing me about the date of his arrival. It was Raja. He brought the biplane all the way from Allahabad for me. I laughed, trying to infuse a lot of sarcasm into it. I told him I was not a child to be taken in by the likes of him. I was in the midst of my examinations. I was a girl who knew her responsibilities. I said goodbye but didn't move, waiting for him to beat a retreat like a dog kicked out. Softly smiling, he said, what if I gave the exams a slip?' I walked out proudly to impress on him that I would not be such an easy conquest. I washed my face, changed into a fresh saree, and came out. Why? Why didn't I sit in my room and start preparing for the exam? On the morrow?

Did I know he would be waiting there for me?

Did I nurture a secret desire that he should be there waiting for me?

Did I wish he would go away and relieve me of this uncertainty?

Then a round over the city of Banaras in the biplane. Sitting beside him, floating amidst the clouds. Looking down at the Ganga, the pillars of Aurangzeb, and the semi-circular university campus. Getting happily checked by the fast-moving wind.

Then marriage in the Registrar's office in Allahabad. Giving the go-by to exams. Raja is losing his job. Grounds for his dismissal: Instead of training pilots, he went about flying a girlfriend at the expense of the training centre. Then the return to Madras.

He got a job in the Madras Flying Club. Father, who looked at us with a deep frown on his forehead, ultimately softened, heaved a sigh, even smiled and blessed both of us in English. Trying to pierce through a cloud, the plane loses height and then settles down again.

The hostess, with a huge pile of trays in her hands, sways like a drunk and almost falls into the lap of a passenger. The passenger stretches his hands in a brave effort to catch her if she falls or to pull her into his lap if she doesn't. The hostess smiles at the passenger, either indicating that she knows his trick or purely in apology for her failure to fall into his lap. She puts a tray in front of him and moves forward. I nod my head, indicating that I don't want anything. She asks me if she can bring me a glass of lemon juice. I convey my refusal in a smile. I want to tell her, 'Poor Child'. If your husband is lying dead in a faraway place and you are going to see him, you don't feel like eating or drinking.' No, she is not married. Cannot be. Maybe lovers she has. But a lover is no husband. Even if he becomes one, he cannot remain a lover for long. I want to caution her: 'Poor child'. I hear you are agitating for the right to marry. Believe me, a lover is a better proposition than a husband. But until then, why put your life in jeopardy? It is a good thing that the government has decided that you should not get married while in service. The urgency of the need to tell her becomes an acute pain in the stomach. I rest my aching forehead on the front seat. The gentleman sitting beside me becomes nervous on my account. His sense of decorum prevents him from asking me if I need help. His desire to call the hostess and ask her to find if there is a doctor on board the plane is evident in the spasmodic movement of his hands and knees. I reassure him that there is nothing wrong with me: I lean back against the seat smiling. Nothing, a small mishap. Last night my husband died suddenly. That's all. If I put it into words, it will sound terrible to the gentleman. So, I indicate it through a smile. Forty minutes still. One cannot even jump out of a plane. Even if they stretch into forty hours or even aeons, one has to wait patiently.

Waiting for him patiently had become an important part of my life.

He would promise he would come back by eight. I would wait, looking at the clock. Eight... Nine... Ten... Twelve. He would come back sometime during the small hours of the morning. I would pretend to be asleep and wait for him to wake me up, my stomach painfully empty with hunger. He would lie down beside me and go to sleep, while I would spend sleepless hours nursing my hunger, my resentment, and my head splitting with ache. I spent whole nights, minutes stretching into hours, hours into unmoving eternity. And in the morning, when he took me into his arms and planted that sweet, inimitable kiss on my lips, trying to wipe out all the misery I had felt, I would feel at peace with life, but the small wound of misery in the heart never had time to heal completely; we went about in a hectic spree till it almost healed, but invariably the wound would open again. This healing and bleeding went on and ultimately, though the wounds bled no more, their indelible marks were permanently etched on my heart.

I knew that he had more than mere intimate association with several other women. I wanted to put him in the dock with my proofs but never had the heart to do it. On one occasion I had almost done it. I stayed with my father for a couple of days on the occasion of his sixtieth birthday. Because mother was no more there to look to the arrangements. I had to spend the nights too in my father's house. Raja attended the function, and after dinner we returned home. I put on my nightgown and lifted the pillow to adjust it more conveniently. There was a bra underneath it. I was looking at it. He saw it. I looked at him, and he looked at me. There was a twinkle in his eye, and also apprehension. He drew me into his tight embrace, saying, 'You must have left it there.' I pushed him a little away to be able to see into his eyes and told him in an accusatory tone, 'Not my size. "He didn't show in his looks that there was an implied accusation in what I said. But he knew that I knew.

"I am going to Banaras. I paid the examination fee.

"Why?"

"Then I couldn't finish my exams."

"It was ten years ago. Why do you need a degree now?"

"May come in handy sometime."

He himself bought for me an open return ticket. The day before I left for Banaras, he applied for leave and spent the day with me. We went about the whole city together, making meaningless purchases. Ten days we would not be together. There wouldn't be any opportunity for falling out or making up. The whole day he was telling about himself. He was foolish and selfish and had a fickle mind and no capacity for restraint. Into his aimless meandering life, I came in like a guiding star. The house we built together, the hours we spent together – they were the only things of any permanent value in his life. He would spend these ten days in penance. He would sleep on the floor. He wouldn't drink anything but water. Duty and then home. He wouldn't go out anywhere. He looked like a child when he was saying all this. My eyes became moist. As we were walking to the plane, he asked me all of a sudden, 'Look, why did we decide not to have any children? It was he who insisted on not having any children; he said it would take away half the pleasure of married life. He himself brought the pills.' If you go away somewhere like this, how can I spend time all alone? If we have a boy or a girl, they'll fill the gap.' 'Even now it's not too late. I'm thirty, and you are thirty-two,' I said in a choking voice. Suddenly I felt like staying away. Let the exams go to hell. I would give up using the pills from that day, and before the end of the year, there would be a baby in my arms. I was standing in the doorway of the plane, and they were pulling the stepladder away. I felt an urgent desire to jump down and run into his arms. They closed the doors. I ran to the seat and looked through the window. He saw me, and we made so many promises to each other by waving our hands. Now, we are so far removed from each other that we have no chance of fulfilling even one of those promises. Suddenly I feel I'm falling into an abyss, as though there is nothing to support my feet, as though the seat beneath me has suddenly disappeared. The plane is landing. Raja explained and demonstrated to me several times about zero gravity in his trainer plane. As the plane loses altitude, your body becomes light as a feather, as though it has no existence.

Even the mind becomes devoid of all feeling. Not even the burden of thought you feel. You become a piece of cotton, a feather. On either side of the plane, there are banks of dead, unmoving clouds hanging by virtue of inertia. How fine it would be if one could just become inert like them, static and unfeeling. But even clouds are in turmoil on occasions; then they roar angrily and expend their energies in blinding flashes. All at once, they melt; their hearts become heavy and they fall to the earth in torrents.

As the landing gear touches the earth, I become conscious of my enormous weight; I am falling forward with tonnes of momentum, and the belt is holding me back to the seat. The muscles of my lower abdomen constrict in unbearable pain. The plane has stopped, and the muscles relax a little. I sit in the seat as light and static as a cloud. I don't loosen the belt until all of them got down. No, I will not cause the poor hostess any more anxiety. I remove the belt and get up. I walk on my legs as though they are not mine, and the mind too has become light, as a feather. As I get down, the hostess smiles and folds her hands in farewell. A little away from the steps, I see Dr Natarajan and Father.

Father hurries up the steps and takes me into his embrace. I pretend to shed tears from my dried-up eyes, hiding my face on his shoulder. From the emptiness inside me, not even tears come out. Then everyone has come to know that I am the wife of Captain Raja – the hostesses and the traffic staff.

The ground staff know about it already because my father and Dr Natarajan have come to receive me. The car is brought nearer the steps, and we get in; Dr Natarajan in the front seat, and Father and I in the back seat. I look back at the aeroplane through the rear window.

I saw the hostess talking to the pilot in wide-eyed wonder; probably she is saying, 'I didn't know she was Mrs Raja. That was why she was like that all through the journey. Had she known, what else could she have done? The wood rose creeper has spread out wildly on the portico. The drumstick tree in the corner of the yard, which I planted disregarding the objections of Raja, is infested with caterpillars. I feel dizzy as the car stops. Father lends me the support of his arm. I don't want to get down; don't want to go in; want to get back to the airport, to Banaras, to go through with the unfinished exams. Raja is lying down on his favourite divan in the hall. The flower garland around his neck is petrified on the dry ice. On the wall opposite, his smiling living photo. On the divan, he was permanently frozen. As I step nearer, Father holds me back. Dr Natarajan stands in between me and the body as though to protect it.

I look at him.

'Post-mortem had to be done,' he said. 'Isn't it a heart attack?'

'On account of some suspicious circumstances. It was heart attack really, thank god'. As though dying of a heart attack is a virtue. I look at him questioningly. Then I see Rahamtulla – the circle inspector. I can't bring myself to ask him any questions. I go into the bedroom. The double bed looks repulsive. I go into the bathroom and fill the tub with steaming water. Father's anxiety as to what I would do. I reassure him through a smile and close the bathroom doors. I lie down in the scalding water for hours.

Father and the rest of them return from the electric crematorium. Four o'clock. Rahamatulla comes in, hesitates, not knowing how to tell me. It seems Raja was lying dead near the bathroom door when the gardener saw him in the morning. He rang up, and Dr Natarajan and Father came there. He must have died some hours earlier, probably sometime around 2 a.m. But the rear door was open, and the gardener came into the house that way, wondering why it was open.

Doctor felt that the police should be called in, and so he came. He made a thorough search and found this jewel case. And this bill for Rs. 652.30. But the jewel case was empty. So, he had to question the servants. A necklace was found... in the house of the servant maid Thalupulu. So, a post-mortem had to be ordered. Thalupulu maintained that Raja himself had given it to her the previous night; he assured her it was gilded and not the real thing. But the shopkeeper said it was 14-carat gold; Raja purchased it a couple of days ago. They can charge Thalupulu with the theft. If she gives a written complaint, he will arrest Thalapulu.

But.... I go into the bedroom. Raja's photo is on the bedside table. We purchased that ivory frame in

Mysore. I have a silent session with the photo. If Thalupulu is brought to the court, she will maintain that he spent the night with her and gave her the necklace. That must have been the truth. A truth I cannot imagine even as plausible. If it were some air hostess or telephone operator, it would be understandable. But Thalupulu? Had he fallen so low as to ... No.... He dragged me down to that level... to the level of Thalupulu. I was just another woman like Thalupulu so far as he was concerned. But she has no share, like me, in the rest of his things; this house, his car, this furniture, the yard, the garden... But the double bed? It is as much hers as mine... And his person too.

I feel dizzy. Want to lie down... no, not on that bed... the bed which he shared with her that one night... maybe several nights. I sit on the stool in front of the dressing table. Slowly Thalupulu comes in, pushing open the door, her hands shivering. She closes the door. I look at her. Her saree is worn tight around her knees, exposing her lovely muscular calf muscles, dark like black ivory, full and vital. Her breasts bursting out of her blouse. Her eyes waver out of fear. I get up slowly. He had given the necklace to her, and so it is hers. I said I give her the jewel case too. She puts the necklace on the dressing table, indicating she doesn't want it.

Raja Babu said it was gilded. He lied. It was a little past midnight... I said I would go home. He asked me to go through the rear door. He said he would close it himself... I never, never thought he would cheat all of us like this..."

She breaks down into sobs, unable to speak any further. I want to stretch my arms and hug her to my bosom. Torrents of agony will flow, drenching us both in a single burst. Who knows who is counselling whom? He is lost to both of us. Alive, he dragged me down to the level of Thalupulu; dead, he brings Thalupulu to my level.

"Get out", I literally shout her out of the room. His disembodied look from the photo on the bedside table fills me with loneliness. He is beyond any accusations or expectations, far, far away.

Translated by Shri Palagummi Padmaraju
(Rendered from the original story Kolavarani Dooram in Telugu)

CHAPTER XIV

Disillusioned

I

Kamala was going to the tank to fetch water; her right arm wound itself round the neck of the polished brass vessel, which rested on her projecting hip, and she bent gracefully to her left to balance herself. The bulging portion of the vessel exactly fit into the shapely, deep curve of her waist, and its colour matched with that of her half-uncovered back. Her slim figure swung this way and that as she walked slowly on the rugged, uneven street of the village, which was deeply furrowed by the age-long traffic of bullock carts.

As she passed on, noticing every house almost absent-mindedly, a sight in one of the houses suddenly attracted her. The husband was obviously going to the fair in a neighbouring village. The wife was standing, one leg lightly resting upon the doorway, her whole weight balanced on the other, and a plump child on her hip. The husband was teasing her with a half-serious refusal of something. His wife, in affected seriousness, threatened him, "I won't cook food for you if you don't get what I want." "We shall see about that," he replied, forcing down a smile that threatened to light upon his lips. The wife, anyhow, could not control herself and laughed out merrily.

Kamala was neither looking at him nor at her but was watching the entire situation with all the meaning behind it, the universality of the relations of men and women, of which this was but a phase. There were fifty houses in that street, and in each house a man and a woman united by marriage, but the meaning of marriage she never knew. To her, it appeared that the whole society, and in fact the whole world, was built upon the foundation of marriage. A husband and a wife were the unit, the ultimate atom of society. But to her, the relations between a man and a woman were as abstract and unknown as the electrical forces that hold the atom intact. She only knew that they were there. Her sparkling eyes were always directed to some region beyond all these men and women, beyond the horizon, breaking into the mist that hid the heaven of married love. Her smile was neither happy nor melancholy, but it was there on her full, round lips, eternally.

She had been married at the age of eight, and she was twenty-five now. Two years after she was married, her husband ran away somewhere, and her people could not spot him out in the vastness of the world. After twelve years, she was duly declared a widow. But the peculiar circumstances that made her a widow left her in a confusion as to her real position in life. She could not believe that she was a widow. With women who knew that their husbands were dead, it was different. But her husband did not die, at least not before her eyes, and nobody saw him die as far as her knowledge went. She always thought of him, and thoughts of him almost became second nature to her.

She got down the steps into the tank and let the vessel float on the water. She went in till the water was neck deep, throwing the end of her saree over the vessel, and it followed her wherever she went, like a dumb dog its master. Her face was almost hidden in the thickly grown lotuses, some white, some red. Their mild scent possessed her. Some were so ripe that their petals collapsed at the mere touch. As she moved this way and that, they rubbed against her rosy cheeks. For a moment she imagined that a man, her man, was caressing her. She had vague notions of how a man would fold a woman in his strong arms, rubbing his manly cheeks against hers. She wanted to be in the tank like that forever, but she was reminded of her work at home. She got up with a deep sigh and retraced her steps back to the house, her vessel full, the same thoughts in her eyes. The wet cloth clung to her golden body, and she felt a mild shudder.

She experienced that something was possessing her all over. She came home and cooked the food for the family. This was almost her routine every day. Thus, she would daily go to the tank, observing the husbands and the wives of the village, bathe there amidst the lotuses, come home, and cook food for the family. For seven years her physical environment was rice, curries, fire, salt, and chilies.

Work became such a routine to her that she would never put too much salt in a curry, nor overcook the rice, despite her absent-mindedness. Her legs got accustomed to the street that led to the tank, and her hands to the work of the day. She did not bestow even a little thought on anything. Her physical frame performed all its duties with mechanical perfection. But her mind always dwelt in some distant heaven with which she was but little acquainted. Even when she slept, her thoughts were awake. It was fifteen years ago, and she did not remember how she felt then. Her father wept over her once or twice, crying that she was doomed in life. But then, it did not mean anything to her.

She vaguely felt that something went wrong somewhere but never knew that all her future was condemned to a life of isolation in a kitchen, with nobody to think or feel strongly about her. The same father who wept for her confined her to the kitchen and called her a widow. He grew angry if she failed to do her duty well. She had sisters, whose arrival in the house was welcome, and brothers, all of whom were married. There was something about all these people that society respected. She was not on the same footing as they, while yet a girl. What made this difference? Her girlfriends would always talk to her about their husbands. What was a husband?

The difference in treatment she received at the hands of society made it clear to her that a husband was a sort of refuge for a woman and that with a husband a woman could flourish in society like a flower in spring. A woman owed everything, her position, her nature, and even her individuality, to her husband. This was what Kamala understood life to be. If society respected the individuality of a woman apart from her husband, then only could a widow be regarded with the respect she deserved.

And so, she clung to him, though only in thought, desperately. And she found her solace. For twelve years she was neither a widow nor a girl with a husband, and now she was a widow.

Three years ago, she was told that now, irrevocably, she was a widow. She did not know how the change came about. Her position in society did not change, neither did her state of mind. Society said there was a change; that was all. But she never regarded herself as a widow. From the very day when, in her, a youthful buoyancy sprang up, she thought of him incessantly, and years could not slacken that attachment. She never grew desperate about her future. Women of her age already had two or three children and were looking quite a lot older than she. She felt she was young, and the cool breezes made her blood tingle in her round limbs. Her uncoiled curls of hair became brown but were not out of place behind a light-yellow face tinted a little pink. She felt the fullness of her body with a certain pride and could not believe that it was all doomed to the drudgery of a kitchen. She felt that there was something yet in store for her. One day the doors of heaven would suddenly fling themselves open. And years would not exhaust that bliss. She never doubted the possibility. She had no idea of how her husband looked. Her people said he was a fine young man. Of course, he must have been. There was his photo in one of the rooms of the house, and she saw it once or twice when nobody was there. The photo did not tell her anything extraordinary, and he was quite a common-looking man, but she felt that his looks were cool and kind and revealed an innate goodness of heart. Surely, she thought, this man was incapable of deceiving anybody or of being wantonly cruel. He would come back to her one day from the vastness of the world, searching her out in every nook and corner. He would find her out and call her away, away to some far-off heaven, far from all this drudgery and all the dullness of the world around her.

Time rolled on in this manner. Days, months, and years passed by unnoticed. But her thoughts remained the same. Daily the same routine, both on the mental and the physical planes. She dwelt in perpetual thought but never grew weary of it. The youthful spirit in her seemed to gain something day by day. She always looked into the future for some day that did not come, and yet she never grew desperate. Enough years had elapsed in that dry environment to parch up the very fountain of youth. But she was different and would not so easily give in. She did not care what people said about her. As far as she was concerned, she did not know when her husband ran away. For her, he existed somewhere and would return to her someday.

II

That day there was nobody in the house. The men were off to the fields, and the women went to attend a marriage in that village. Kamala was all alone, in the company only of her own thoughts. Her dreamy eyes were half closed, and her head drooped to a side slightly as she sat leaning against a pillar.

In, came a man with a dark moustache. He looked like a man of thirty. There was confusion in his look, and he seemed to get excited with every step that brought him nearer to her. She stood up, adjusting her saree, and asked, "Whom do you want? "He did not reply immediately but got all the more confused. A slight tremor was visible all over him. He stammered out, "Are you K-Kamala? "She started at the question and stared at him in dumb surprise, replying in a whisper, "Y-Y-Yes."

He dropped his head till it touched his chest, not daring to look into her eyes. Tears glittered in his eyes. He slowly said, "I am your husband."

She clasped her hands on her swelling bosom and closed her eyes for a blissful moment. After all, he came, but she knew he would be coming. The heaven of which she dreamt so long was near at hand. She felt her little heart too weak to bear the joy. She could not doubt at all that it might not be him. Of course, there was little resemblance between him and that photo. But the kind look was the same, and the photo was fifteen years younger. She told herself that it was at the same face that she had stolen a secret glance, lifting her face a little from its rest on her left knee, on the day of her marriage. Oh, what happiness! Now these fifteen years seemed to her but a split second, and her bliss was one continuous rhapsody, from the day of her marriage to some future eternity. She dared not look into his face but stood there absorbed in joy. She had left the desert behind, and here was the beautiful oasis....

All rejoiced at his coming back. Kamala began her life anew. The new chapter in her life was all promise. But now, she felt, it was by a mere accident that she came into this new life. She dreamt of a heaven all her life, but it was only a dream, and now she realized how foolish it was of her to have placed so much confidence in her dreams. And yet it was good in a way. It kept her alive, alive and young, with all the bloom of a young rose, which ceased to grow after opening its petals. She was all excitement and pitied those innumerable human beings who never realize their dreams and die dreaming to the last moment. God was very partial to her, but God was himself limited by his sense of justice. She could not attribute the cause to anything, not even to her good fortune.

III

"I am going to town. Is there anything I can bring you?" asked her husband.

"For me? "What could she want? She did not know.

"Yes, for you." "I don't want anything."

"Oh, come, come.... Are you cross with me?"

"Why do you think so?"

"You look so out of sorts today."

"I simply don't want anything. That's all."

If he could not understand that much! Long days and nights she had dreamt of him, and at last he had come. What reason did he have to think that she was cross with him?

He did not seem satisfied with her present mood and walked away.

She sat there musing.

"Is there anything I can bring for you?" ......

She did not know what to answer. She did not know what she wanted. What did she want? Perhaps nothing. What did she expect of life? Perhaps nothing—now. Once it was different. She did not know what a husband ought to be or what a husband meant to most others. But life to her was certainly not what she thought it should have been. It was not exactly this that she had dreamt of all her days. That heaven, she felt, must be something very different. She could not make up her mind as to how her husband should behave. He always put on an air of obedience, was afraid of her slightest change of mood, and hesitated at the threshold of each moment of familiarity. She knew that he would give her everything, even his very life, for the asking. But this was not what she wanted. She was prepared to dedicate her whole life to him the moment she found him. But here he was, incapable of accepting anything from her. Instead, he offered her everything. And she was dissatisfied. There was only just a mild excitement in her new life. It appeared to her, by and by, that the life she was leading now was not materially different from the life she had led before. The same house, the same environment, the same street leading to the same tank, and the same cooking were all there still. But these did not belong to the heaven she was once dreaming of. She saw people around her who were perfectly happy. It was surprising that there were so many contented faces in the world. There were many women who were proud of their husbands and looked it too, every moment of their lives.

How was her husband to behave? What did she want of him? Why did he appear to her so promising before he actually came to her? And what made this difference? She knew there were mean and cruel men in the world. Her husband was extremely good-natured. But he was somehow not the man she was expecting him to be. By his very virtues, so to speak, he fell short of her expectations. She thought she would be relieved of all this drudgery. But there it remained, even now. Women, widowed or otherwise, had to fetch water from the tank and had to cook. Did she not know before that woman cook for their husbands? Then how could she think that she would be relieved of her monotonous duties?

How were other women able to put up with life at all? How happy she once was, always dreaming! How pleasant it was, just to hope! But here was the obvious fulfillment of her hopes, and here she was, the victim of that very fulfillment. She almost hated herself.

IV

"Kamala, is hot water ready for me? "

"No."

"Why? Didn't you put water in the boiler?" "No. I forgot. I am sorry."

But she did not look sorry at all, because she had not really forgotten. She had deliberately not prepared hot water for her husband. An unconquerable malice in her wanted to offend him, insult him, and take revenge on him—but for what sin of his she knew not, and she cared not to know.

"How could you forget, Kamala? I told you I had to go out very early today. "

"You did not tell me."

"I did. And you just now said yourself you had forgotten. I told you last night." "You did not, "she flared back, with unusual vehemence.

"You did not, and.... oh, you are taking the very life out of me. She started weeping. He came to her, full of kindness.

"Did I say anything harsh to you, Kamala? Forgive me if I did. Don't be unhappy." He put on a penitent face, as if he were the guilty party! She was still sobbing. He tried to soothe her. She suddenly stopped weeping and said in a mild voice, almost pleadingly, "Why did you come back into my life at all? It was nice once, when you were away. You should never have returned. I was so carefree before you came." He put one of his hands on her shoulder and with the other tried to lift her face to his. She slowly released herself and went into her room, closing the door behind her. She threw herself on her bed and wept aloud as in great agony. He did not try to follow her but stood where she left him and heaved a deep sigh. It was the most miserable day of her existence. She was too full of shame and misery to look any human being in the face. The next morning, she found that her husband had left her again. There was a small note from him in which was written merely this: "I am going away. Don't search for me." The whole household began to weep. All her relatives cursed him, exclaiming that they always knew he was such a fellow. Kamala wept too, but she did not know why exactly she was weeping. She only knew it was not, this time, because her husband had left her and gone away.

- Translated by Shri Palagummi Padmaraju
(Rendered from the original story in Telugu)

PALAGUMMI PADMARAJU

Published in Triveni magazine—1939

167

Literary Works

Of

Shri.Palagummi Padmaraju

(Telugu)

<u>Short Stories written by</u>

<u>Palagummi Padmaraju</u>

(Telugu)

1. Subbi

2. Balyam

3. Pantham

4. Kurrathanama? Manava Swabhavama?

5. Oka Sanghatana

6. Theerthaputudrekalu

7. Udvegaalu

8. Cheekatlo Merupulu

9. Pulli

10. Maayajulu

11. Padava Prayanam

12. Coolie Janam

13. Mugguru Mithrulu

14. Vasana leni Poovulu

15. Rangayya

16. Mussulivadi Parichayam

17. Eduru choosthunna Muhurtham

18. Gaalivana

19. Phalashruti

20. Viyyanna Thatha Maranam

21. Evarikevaru

22. Paalapongu

23. Veerayya Veera Maranam

24. Kota Godalu

25. Mogapurushudu Aadastri

26. Issaka Thinnelu

27. Khandasari Chekkara Kasimajilelu

28. Illu Ammakam

29. Vendi Sisa

30. Ghoramaina Neram

31. Deyyala Garuvu

32. Manavulantha Sodarulena

33. Chintha Chachina

34. Adugujadalu

35. Ranga Bhoomi

55. Cinema (Ki) Katha

56. Railu Pettelo

57. Ramasubbu Leelalu Rangaprasada Mardhanam

58. Vaana Vachina Rathri

59. Aasajeevulu

<u>Translation Works written by</u>

<u>Palagummi Padmaraju</u>

(Telugu)

1. Champabadina Agyapathram - Originally written by Li. Kinger (German)
2. Vechathanam Kosam Anveshana - Originally written by Joseph Margin Bar (German)
3. Theeratha Yathra - Originally written by Hans Bender (German)
4. Aa Mangalvaram Nadu - Originally written by Johann Wolfgang von Goethe (German)
5. Swecha Prantham - Originally written by Hubert Fichte (German)
6. Aakupacha Lady Charmam - Originally written by Gerd Gaiser (German)
7. Karmika Sangha Sabhyudu - Originally written by Max von der Grun (German)

He translated some of his short stories in English and he also translated works from American literature.

<u>Novels written by</u>

<u>Palagummi Padmaraju</u>

(Telugu)

1. Batikina College

2. Nalla Regadi

3. Ramarajyaniki Rahadaari

4. Rendo Ashokudi Munalla Palana

5. Chachi Saadhinchaadu

6. Bhakta Sabari

7. Chachi Poyina Manishi

Poetry written by

Palagummi Padmaraju

1. Prema navvithe

2. Jeevana swargam

3. Aa Remma

4. Naa Paata

5. Raave Preyasi

6. Cheekati

7. Maa palle

8. Neevu-Nenu

9. Ninduchoolu

10. Puriti paata

11. Godavari

12. Bhoomi!oh Bhoomi

13. Pedakaapu

14. Aa voore vaipu?

15. Errajeera

16. Ee Raathri

17. Nisilo nijam

Story written by

Palagummi Padmaraju for movies: -

(Telugu)

1. Bangaru Papa - 1955
2. Bhagya Rekha - 1957
3. Santhi Nivasam -1960 (This was based on Palagummi Padmaraju's popular stage play 'Santhi Nivasam'.)
4. Bhakta Sabari - 1960
5. Bikari Ramudu - 1961
6. Rangula Ratnam - 1967
7. Bangaru Panjaram - 1969
8. Vaikuntapali - 1975

9. Mana Voori Katha - 1976
10. Swapna -1980
11. Pralaya Rudrudu – 1982
12. Haalu Jenu -1982 (Kannada)
13. Bahudoorapu Batasari - 1983
14. Illale Devata -1985 (Remake of Kannada film Haalu Jenu)
15. Stri – 1995

("On the boat" short story was made into a movie, directed by K.Sethumadhavan)

<u>Dialogues written by</u>

<u>Palagummi Padmaraju for movies: -</u>

(Telugu)

1. Bangaru Papa - 1955
2. Bhagya Rekha - 1957
3. Vegu Chukka -1957
4. Bhakta Sabari 1960
5. Kalanthakudu -1960
6. Papala Bhairavudu -1961
7. Sri Krishna Kuchela - 1961
8. Gopaludu Bhupaludu - 1967
9. Devuni Gelichina Manavadu - 1967
10. Sukha Duhkhalu - 1968
11. Bangaru Panjaram - 1969
12. Circar Express -1968
13. Chuttarikalu - 1968
14. Grama Devathalu - 1968
15. Paala Manasulu - 1968
16. Maa Nanna Nirdoshi - 1970
17. Bhale Etthu Chivariki Chitthu -1970

18. Oke Kutumbam - 1970
19. Manchivallaku Manchivadu -1973
20. Aajanma Brahmachari - 1973
21. Vaikunthapali (1975)
22. Sri Raja Rajeswari Vilas Coffee Club - 1976

<u>Dubbed Movies written by</u>

<u>Palagummi Padmaraju for movies: -</u>

1. Marmayogi -1951 (Tamil)
2. Parasakthi -1952 (Tamil) – Parasakthi (Telugu)
3. Bhagdad Thirudan -1960 (Tamil) – Bhagdad Gajadonga

(Telugu)

<u>Lyrics written by</u>

<u>Palagummi Padmaraju for movies: -</u>

(Telugu)

<u>Bhakta Ambareesha -1959</u>

1. Kari Makarula
2. Ee Na Kesa (Poem)
3. Sri Maha Vishnudeva (Poem)
4. Nanne Manambumlo

<u>Bhaktha Sabari - 1960</u>

1. Rama Nyayama
2. Bhavatharaka
3. Pandina Dehamu(Poem)
4. Huha Huha
5. Thali Na Apradham(Poem)
6. Aalu Magalu

<u>Bikari Ramudu -1961</u>

1. Challani nee daya
2. Aey Papamu erugani
3. Vadena Cheli
4. Nidhuramma
5. Ee Dinam Naa Manam
6. Yechata nundi vachavo

<u>Sri Krishna Kuchela - 1961</u>

1. Brindavihara
2. Moodulokaala
3. Swagatham Edhe
4. Kanula Kunuku Ledu
5. Paavana Thulasi Maatha
6. Sri Ramani Ramana
7. Adigina Yentha
8. Namithi Na Manambuna
9. Nandha Yashoda
10. Nilupamjalanu
11. Kannayya
12. Hey Gopaalaa
13. Prama Pavithrudaina

14. Dallmainanu Pushapamainanu
15. Koluvai Yundena
16. Gopala Hey Krupavala

<u>Devatha- 1965</u>

1. Bhalare Dheeruda

<u>Bhoolokamlo Yamalokam -1966</u>

1. Balavanthudu Gurramupai-
2. Akka Bhartaku Seelamarpimpa
3. Hitamu Koredu Purohitunatlu
4. Bhethala Shakti Kalpinchina Neevu

<u>Gopaludu Bhoopaludu - 1967</u>

1. Ekkadi Vaado

<u>Bhaktha Prahladha - 1967</u>

1. Janani Varadayini Trilochani

<u>Sri Raja Rajeswari Vilas Coffee Club - 1976</u>

1. Rakoyi Anukoni Athidhi

<u>Buchi Babu -1980</u>

1. Panchadhara Valana Palu Rogamulu Vachu
2. Sevakulaku Hotel Serverlakunu
3. Valapu Jwaramunaku Dhavada Paguluta Mandhu

<u>Mega Sandesam - 1982</u>

1. Priye Charuseele - Jayadevudu
2. Poems

<u>Screenplay written by</u>

<u>Palagummi Padmaraju for movies: -</u>

(Telugu)

1. Raja Makutam - 1960

   B.N. Reddy, Palagummi Padmaraju

2. Sukha Duhkhalu - 1968

<u>Direction by</u>

<u>Palagummi Padmaraju for movies: -</u>

(Telugu)

1. Bikari Ramudu - 1961

(This was debut movie for Palagummi Padmaraju as a director.)

2. Devudu Ichchina Bhartha - 1968

   Marmayogi -1951 (Tamil)

   Parasakthi -1952 (Tamil) – Parasakthi (Telugu)

   Bhagdad Thirudan -1960 (Tamil) – Bhagdad Gajadonga

<u>Filmography</u>

1. Marmayogi -1951 (Dubbed Movie)
2. Parasakthi -1952 (Dubbed Movie)
3. Bangaru Papa - 1955
4. Rakatha Kanneru - 1956
5. Bhagya Rekha - 1957
6. Vegu Chukka -1957
7. Bhakta Ambareesha - 1959
8. Santhi Nivasam - 1960
9. Raja Makutam - 1960
10. Bhakta Sabari - 1960
11. Kalanthakudu -1960
12. Bhagdad Gajadonga – 1960 (Dubbed Movie)
13. Papala Bhairavudu -1961
14. Sri Krishna Kuchela -1961
15. Bikari Ramudu - 1961
16. Devatha - 1965
17. Bhoolokamlo Yamalokam - 1966
18. Rangula Ratnam - 1967
19. Bhaktha Prahaladha - 1967
20. Gopaludu Bhupaludu - 1967

21. Devuni Gelichina Manavadu - 1967
22. Sukha Duhkhalu - 1968
23. Circar Express -1968
24. Chuttarikalu - 1968
25. Grama Devathalu - 1968
26. Devudichchina Bharta - 1968
27. Paala Manasulu - 1968
28. Bangaru Panjaram - 1969
29. Maa Nanna Nirdoshi - 1970
30. Bhale Etthu Chivariki Chitthu -1970
31. Oke Kutumbam - 1970
32. Manchivallaku Manchivadu - 1973
33. Aajanma Brahmachari - 1973
34. Vaikuntapali - 1975
35. Sri Raja Rajeswari Vilas Coffee Club - 1976
36. Mana Voori Katha - 1976
37. Buchi Babu -1980
38. Swapna - 1980
39. Mega Sandesam - 1982
40. Pralaya Rudrudu - 1982
41. Bahudoorapu Batasari - 1983
42. Illale Devata -1985
43. Stri – 1995